**He was a stranger, her husband.
A man she barely knew...**

"You are quite lovely. Your eyes are beautiful," he said. His voice had dropped several tones. His change of mood startled her.

"It's kind of you to...tell me so."

He laughed. "A polite response...but I am not being kind, only honest." He moved closer to her and caressed her cheek. His touch was light but it awakened pulses that sped through her body. She wanted to say something but shyness stayed her tongue. He was very close to her now—and of a sudden, he gathered her gently in his arms and bore her to the bed...

Dear Reader,

Your enthusiastic reception of SECOND CHANCE AT LOVE has inspired all of us who work on this special romance line and we thank you.

Now there are *six* brand new, exciting SECOND CHANCE AT LOVE romances for you each month. We've doubled the number of love stories in our line because so many readers like you asked us to. So, you see, your opinions, your ideas, what you think, really count! Feel free to drop me a note to let me know your reactions to our stories.

Again, thanks for so warmly welcoming SECOND CHANCE AT LOVE and, please, *do* let me hear from *you*!

With every good wish,

Carolyn Nichols
SECOND CHANCE AT LOVE
The Berkley/Jove Publishing Group
200 Madison Avenue
New York, New York 10016

Second Chance at Love
REGENCY

AN ADVERSE ALLIANCE
LUCIA CURZON

SECOND CHANCE AT LOVE
BOOK

First edition published February 1982

First printing

"Second Chance at Love" and the butterfly emblem are trademarks belonging to Jove Publications, Inc.

Printed in the United States of America

Second Chance at Love books are published by
The Berkley/Jove Publishing Group,
200 Madison Avenue, New York, NY 10016

Part One

1

ALL WAS BUSTLE, confusion, and recriminations in Heberdeen House, the town residence of Sir Bertram Heberdeen, for preparations were underway for the first ball the master had given since being invalided home from Waterloo eleven months earlier. Indeed, it was the first such entertainment to have graced the mansion in over a decade.

For most of the preceding week a small staff of servants, augmented by recruits from The Corners, the Heberdeen country estate, had been cleaning, polishing, waxing, dusting, and airing the furnishings, floors, and walls of the immense rooms which had been closed off for the better part of four years. Miss Anthea Heberdeen, Sir Bertram's sister, and the elderly cousin who served as her companion, had spent most of their time in the back parlor, the library, and their bedchambers until Sir Bertram's return necessitated the opening of his suite. However, despite the feverish activity which had already prevailed, much remained to be done.

It was a hectic day. More than once, Mrs. Niker, the housekeeper, had been heard to mutter distractedly that she ought to 'ave been given more notice concerning the ball. None dared remind the formidable lady there had been plenty of notice and that she—too used to playing patience and quaffing brandy in her rooms—did not heed such notice until practically the last moment. That was not entirely Mrs. Niker's fault for, in caring for her brother, Miss Anthea had assumed a great many of the duties which normally would have fallen to the housekeeper and, indeed, as morning dwindled into afternoon, it was Miss Anthea's name rather than Mrs. Niker's which was on the lips of nervous housemaids engaged in readying the two drawing rooms and of footmen working in the ballroom.

The lady in question was, however, in the library, closeted with her brother, who at her behest was lying on the daybed put there for his comfort once he was able to come downstairs. Though he had professed himself to be in fine fettle, his sister, used to his every look, had ignored his protests and sternly ordered him to rest.

"If you'll read to me, I shall," he had responded.

Consequently Miss Heberdeen, curled in the huge Queen Anne chair purchased by her great-grandfather, obediently read from her brother's favorite comedy, *The Beggar's Opera*. She had reached the scene where a distraught Polly Peachum had come to visit her highwayman husband MacHeath in prison, only to find him with Lucy Lockit, the jailor's handsome daughter.

"'Where is my dear husband? Was a rope ever intended for this neck? Why dost thou turn away from me? 'Tis thy Polly; 'tis thy wife.'" Anthea's big blue eyes were full of distress, but she narrowed them as, in a deeper voice, she muttered, "'Was there ever such an unfortunate rascal as I am?'" Then her tones turned plaintive and just a touch shrewish for Lucy Lockit's, "'Was there ever such a villain?'

"'Oh, MacHeath,'" she was the distressed Polly again, "'was it for this we parted. Taken, imprisoned, hanged! Cruel reflection. I'll stay with thee till death; no force shall tear thy dear wife from thee now. What means my love?'" Her eyes were puzzled. "'Not one kind word? Not one kind look? Think what thy Polly suffers, to see thee in this condition.'

"'I must disown her,'" Anthea growled MacHeath's aside and then more loudly proclaimed to suspicious Lucy Lockit, "'The wench is distracted!'" Anthea closed the book. "I cannot read any more. I must see how they are progressing in the ballroom."

"Blast the ballroom. I should rather concentrate on the misfortunes of MacHeath." Sir Bertram smiled. "I have said and will say once more, my love, that Aunt Dolly is right— you do have a marked talent for interpretation."

She threw him a fond but doubtful look. "You refine upon it too much, my dearest. Compared with a real professional actress, I am sure my efforts would be found sadly wanting." She sighed. "I do wish Aunt Dolly might be with us tonight."

"I, too," he agreed, adding a trifle defensively, "but 'twas her decision."

"'Twas Society's decision," Anthea retorted. "Yet, for all the Polite World sneers at actresses, it is highly fashionable for a gentleman to choose his mistress from their ranks." Laughing, she put a hand over her mouth. "But I am not supposed to know about such matters, am I?"

"No," her brother said with mock severity, "you certainly are not." Then his laughter filled the room as she looked down demurely, a finger straying to her lips. "What a travesty of innocence you are. I pray you'll not shock our guests with such faces, love, nor startle them with your frank and pithy observations. I know 'tis your wont."

"Only with you. I am not shy with you."

With some compunction he said, "You should not be

shy with anyone. You are prettier and cleverer than most any female I know. Indeed 'twill be a fortunate man wins you as wife, Anthea."

She rose. "I vow my head will be quite turned if I stay to listen any longer. I must go to the ballroom. I've told them to pay particular attention to the mirrors. You'd not credit the dust upon them and on the chandeliers as well. I beg you, Bertie, try and snatch a bit of sleep." Before he could respond, she had hurried out of the library.

As she went down the corridor toward the ballroom, a rueful smile played about her lips. Her brother was quite confident that at this ball, which was being given in her honor and would serve as her official introduction to Society, she must be an immediate success. His love for her did not take into account that she was old for a debutante—six months past the age of nineteen and possessed neither of outstanding beauty nor a great fortune. For herself, she was quite resigned to being a maiden lady like her Cousin Matilda. If Bertie had not been convinced that it was his long recuperation that had kept her from making the marriage he envisioned for her, she never would have agreed to the ball. It had turned the household topsy-turvy and for naught. She, for one, was quite convinced that it was money spent for nothing!

Yet once she had reached the ballroom and found it bright with the light streaming through its four long windows, its mirrors polished and Mark, the footman, his livery protected by a striped apron, placing new candles in the crystal holders of a chandelier which looked like new, she did feel a surge of excitement. It was not right that this chamber should have been closed so long.

To gaze upon it was to send one's mind back some sixteen years when, as a special privilege, a much smaller Anthea, one who still had difficulty pronouncing her "r's," had come down with her brothers Tony and Bertie to stand for a few moments just inside the door. Tony, already slim and handsome at eight, and six-year-old Bertie, plump like herself, had watched entranced as Mama clad in transparent muslin, a diamond tiara in her curls, went through the intricate paces of a country dance with Papa, so handsome in his plum-colored evening coat with a fall of fine lace at his throat.

All the gentlemen had seemed handsome and all the ladies beautiful to the children. Perhaps they were for the very flower of the *ton* had been present, the Heberdeen Balls being famous. Equally famous were the midnight suppers provided by René, the Parisian chef, eventually snared by the Prince Regent. Oh, it had been such a disappointment to be borne away by Simmy, their nickname for Mrs. Sims, their nurse. Tony, his eye on Mama, had been the most reluctant to leave, but he had yielded—no one had dared dispute Simmy's iron rule, though Tony had vowed he should once he was grown as tall as she.

Anthea smiled and sighed. It all seemed such a long time ago and Tony dead these three years past, slain in battle at Vitoria. How handsome he had looked in his Regimentals and Bertie, too. Her parents had been immensely proud of their two sons. In a sense it was as well they had died before Tony, Papa sickening of a cold which turned into lung congestion and Mama wasting away of some undisclosed complaint which Anthea privately believed to be "heartbreak." Consequently they had been spared the news from Vitoria and also the sight of poor Bertie, shipped home from Waterloo with his left leg amputated at the knee and ill for such a long time afterward from fever and complications. She turned away hastily, shutting the door behind her and wishing she could close away her memories as easily.

Then she tensed, hearing the familiar tapping of her brother's crutch. A moment later he had joined her. "Well, love, are you satisfied?"

"Have you rested enough?" she returned severely, thinking as she looked at him that he was more handsome than he had been before going to war. If suffering had traced new lines across his brow, it had also added a depth of character which had not been there before. Mindful of his question, she opened the door again. "Look at the miracles that have been wrought," she intoned dramatically.

As he obeyed, she was conscious of qualms. Would he remember his parents' dancing on that shining floor, would he recall that he had danced upon it too?

He stood on the threshold for a long moment, while her anxieties increased. At length he turned back, saying, "Yes, it looks very well. I'm glad it's summer. I prefer fresh to hothouse roses and we shall have big baskets of them at either end of the room, unless you think it best to use garlands and drape them over the mirrors."

"Baskets," she said with a note of relief. "The flowers will be in water, then. If they're woven into garlands, they'll wither all too quickly."

"Oh, Anthea," Sir Bertram laughed. "I think you have a soft spot even for the poor roses."

She felt her cheeks grow warm as they always did whenever anyone commented upon the absurdly compassionate nature which prevented her from squashing an insect. "I was only thinking of the appearance," she said defensively. "The looks of the ballroom cannot be improved by drooping blossoms."

"You've a large heart as I should know and others must soon—though I shall be loathe to lose you."

Anthea clicked her tongue. "You needn't think of losing me so soon. If you've convinced yourself that one of those eligible bachelors you've invited will offer for me, I fear you must be sadly disappointed. I am near twenty, after all."

"Which does not make you a hoary ancient. And were it not for me, you could have been launched immediately you left the schoolroom. Instead you've incarcerated yourself behind these walls and devoted yourself to me."

"Which was as I wished," she replied as she stood on tiptoe to kiss his cheek. "Order your roses, love. I must see how preparations for the supper are progressing. And then Madame will be waiting to put the finishing touches upon my gown."

"She's not finished yet and the ball only hours away?"

"Not quite," Anthea pulled a face. "Eet ees zee posee-tioning of zee bows, thees I save for zee last . . . like zee good chef with zee icing for zee cake. Zo!"

His laughter raised a chorus of echoes through the cor-ridor. "Aunt Dolly should hear you!"

"I pray you'll not keep mentioning her," Anthea pro-tested. "I do feel so badly that she'll not come. Her life's been exemplary and when I think of the tales told of the Duchess of Devonshire and Emily Cowper and recall that Aunt Dolly's name is inked from the Family Bible and spoken aloud only by us . . . Not even Tony would ac-knowledge her."

"He was not here long enough to know her," interposed her brother.

"He could have sought her out as you did. I loved Tony and I still miss him—but he had not your sensibility. If . . . but I shall not say it."

"No, do not," he advised. Blue eyes met blue eyes, both mirroring looks of reminiscent sorrow for the brother dead and buried in Spain. No breath of criticism must sully him now.

"I must go to the kitchens."

"I must order the roses."

A half hour later Anthea pivoted before the long glass in her bedchamber. Madame Dupré was sitting back on her heels, her dark, slightly simian features squeezed up in a way that emphasized her resemblance to a wise monkey. Anthea stared dubiously from mantua maker to mirror. "Can you really think that white becomes me?" she asked.

"But of course," Madame said predictably. "Eet ees zee only attire for zee *jeune fille* on the brink of emerging."

"Even when that young girl has spent a precious long

time upon that particular brink?" Anthea demanded, only
to receive a blank look from Madame. She swallowed a
sigh. The woman had dressed so many debutantes that they
must have melded into a single form by now—each to be
clad in lacy creations, frilled and be-bowed, flattering to
fragile, willowy figures such as she, Anthea Heberdeen,
did not possess.

The ruffles designed to provide a hint of fullness to an
immature bosom made her look top-heavy. The skirt, de-
scending from a point just below her armpits, was supposed
to fall straight over a hipless shape to the floor. Her own
overgenerous curves interfered with this design and surely
dead white silk covered with matching sarcenet stitched
here and there with sparkling beads should have lent it a
floating rather than a bouncing effect. She imagined that
the late Lady Heberdeen could have worn such a gown even
at thirty and still remain sylphlike. She herself gave promise of being a very weighty sylph and if it had not been her
first ball, she would have insisted upon a blue gown to
match her eyes and set off her waving golden hair, these
being without doubt her best features. Though her nose and
mouth were well shaped, both looked too small in her plump
face and there was a fullness under her chin which, to her
critical eyes, added at least a decade to her age.

"*C'est merveilleux n'est-ce pas?*" Madame sprang to her
feet and clapped her hands together.

Since it was too late to do anything save agree with her,
Anthea said, "You have made a very beautiful gown, Madame."

"And you will look *ravissante* in it, *mon enfant*."

Meeting Madame's eyes in the glass, Anthea discerned
a faraway look in them. More than ever she was convinced
that the mantua maker was looking at the debutante, rather
than any individual client. Perhaps her vision was even
more limited. It was quite possible that she saw only the
gown itself.

Biting down a rueful laugh, she wished the evening at

an end before it had begun. Undoubtedly Bertie would be disappointed. He had set his heart on her making a conquest of some gentleman who was, she thought with another burgeoning laugh, the counterpart of Madame's debutante—the immutable gallant, the answer to every parent's hope and every girl's dream, who must sweep the said debutante into the land of romance, where only Cinderella and the Sleeping Beauty lived happily ever after.

Dear Bertie was really quite deluded when it came to the people he loved. He thought her beautiful just as he had believed Tony to be a veritable Knight of the Round Table. Her elder brother had not possessed half Bertie's kindness and generosity. He had been cold and aloof during his leaves, patronizing to both Bertie and herself. Though she had grieved for his death, it had not been the terrible agony that had overtaken her during the anguished period when she thought Bertie, too, must succumb.

Poor Bertie, so brave about his loss. Yet it would be very difficult for him tonight when he must sit and watch or repair to the cardroom while everyone was dancing, he who had once been so light on his feet—so graceful a partner to Miss Dorcas Ramsey. At the thought of Dorcas a frown crossed Anthea's face. The young woman had become betrothed to Bertie just before he had left for Waterloo. Once he had returned, he had, with practically his first lucid breath, dictated a letter to Anthea, releasing Dorcas from her vows. "I'll not hold her to a promise she'll not wish to keep," he had said stubbornly.

Once the letter had been sent, there had been no reply, no word at all from the girl which, as far as Anthea was concerned, was just as well. Though Dorcas had always seemed very sweet, Anthea had found her manner cloying and even insincere. She wished that Lord and Lady Ramsey had not accepted the invitation which Bertie, out of a sense of duty to old friends of the family, had felt impelled to send. It was possible that tonight he would learn of Dorcas's marriage to another. She did not know if such an event had taken place; she had not read the *Morning Post* for months, and it was possible that such friends as she had seen had thought it expedient to withhold such information. However, it did seem likely that Dorcas must be wed by now; she was a year older than herself.

"Mademoiselle Heberdeen, do you weesh to remove zee gown?" Madame prompted.

Anthea started slightly. "Please," she responded and flushed, feeling that she had sounded far too grateful for that suggestion. Glancing at her large white shape, she grimaced. She could hope that the gown would be held in the embrace of Bertie's apocryphal gentleman at some moment before the evening ended, but she was by no means sanguine on that subject.

Early in the morning of the day on which the Heberdeen Ball was scheduled to take place, an ample, stylishly gowned lady, who looked to be somewhere in her fifties, was ushered into a salon which formed part of a bachelor apartment in a fine old London mansion. Left to her own devices by an obsequious servitor, she regarded her surroundings with disapproval, surprising under the circumstances, for it was a very pleasant room.

Several round tables set about the chamber bore intricately inlaid boxes and there was a Meissen clown of great delicacy and charm set in a cabinet which also contained some fine Chinese ivories and jades. A collection of miniatures lay on another table near a settee framed in dark wood and covered with a green and white striped satin to match the seats of two chairs and the draperies. The walls were paneled in a light wood and over a marble fireplace, just above a pair of crossed foils, was a portrait in an oval frame. It depicted a smiling girl, whose deeper hue of complexion and dark eyes under black slanting brows together with her clustering ebony curls proclaimed her to be of Latin descent.

The visitor, regarding this portrait, winced and turned away quickly. Then, as she saw the door open, she braced herself. Even though hostilities were at an end and a truce declared these two years past, Lady Cornelia Croydon, Dowager Countess of Vane, was wont to look upon her younger and only remaining son with a reminiscent shudder.

As he entered the room, it was immediately to be seen that there was a strong resemblance between the two of them. Though Titus Croydon, Earl of Vane, was much taller than his mother, being over six feet in height, he had her large dark eyes under well-defined brows, her fine nose, and her determined chin, rendered much more attractive by reason of a deep cleft. His mouth, however, was wider and less thin of lip, and his hair, which grew back from a pronounced widow's peak, was almost as black as his father's had been. From that gentleman he had also inherited the deep waves which had been the envy of Lady Cornelia whose curls were strictly the result of irons and papers. His assets also included broad shoulders, a slender waist, and a leg which showed to advantage in the tight stockinette trousers made fashionable by Beau Brummell.

Surveying her son's handsome person, Lady Cornelia looked uncommonly grim as she said or, rather, proclaimed, "Good morning, Titus. I was beginning to wonder if I might be denied the pleasure of your company."

Raising thin dark brows and speaking with a slight drawl, he responded unsmilingly, "Good morning, Mother. I am sorry you were compelled to wait, but I did not expect you at such an early hour."

"I hope I did not rouse you," she murmured insincerely.

"You did," he replied, "but no matter. Pray sit down and tell me what brings you here."

Sitting on the edge of the settee, Lady Cornelia clasped her gloved hands and looked at her son with a mixture of anger and pleading. "Your Cousin Bartholomew . . ." she began and paused to emit a short angry sigh.

"My cousin Bartholomew?" Drawing up a chair, Titus sat down facing his mother. "Yes, what new folly has he committed now?"

"He has been imprisoned in the Fleet for debt," groaned Lady Cornelia.

The news did not appear to either startle or alarm her son. "Indeed? And you propose to do nothing about it?"

"I have done," she snapped. "An hour since—and a sad state he was in, too, half-fuddled with spirits—Blue Ruin, I have no doubt, for 'tis cheaper than brandy. His wife, whining spiritless creature, was with him, and Osbert, too."

"Osbert?" Titus looked blank.

"Your Second Cousin Osbert, Bartholomew's second son. His eldest son, his namesake, is, if you will remember, in the Navy."

"Indeed? I must admit that I have never made it a practice to keep abreast of Bartholomew's progeny or their doings."

"No more should I," returned his mother, "were it not for the position he occupies as your heir. Will you see Vane overrun by that rascal and his brood? As you know, he already has three sons and two daughters and by the look of his wife, another one expected. All thin, weedy, and chinless. Your father will turn over in his grave. As you know, he could never hear the name Bartholomew Croydon without groaning."

Titus's expressive eyebrows were raised a second time. "You speak, Mother, as though Bartholomew's occupation of Vane were a matter of immediate moment. I feel compelled to assure you that I have no intention of dying to accommodate him."

Lady Cornelia's face darkened. "You have no intention," she echoed. "Did your brother Odo have such an intention? *No*, his new hunter threw him and he broke his neck. In the midst of life . . . as I think I need hardly remind you, Titus."

Her son was seen to wince. "Quite so," he agreed in a low voice.

"I will not contenance that creature at Vane . . . not when it is within your power to prevent it."

Titus looked almost as grim as his mother. "If you are suggesting marriage again, I have no desire to embark upon such a course." He shot a glance at the portrait. "I could not love another."

"Great heavens," Lady Cornelia arose and took a turn around the room, coming back to face her son who had also risen. "It does not matter if you can love, no one is asking you to love . . ."

"It would not be fair . . ."

"Fair?" she countered furiously. "Is it fair that that man live to call Vane his own? Titus, I do not ask the impossible. I do not say that you should even change your mode of life. All I ask is that you remember Vane and ask yourself if you want Bartholomew Croydon slinking through its halls and before long selling off the fine paintings and ancient artifacts to support his gaming at whatever low hell will still receive him—all the good clubs having blackballed him!"

Titus stiffened and was silent a moment, frowning at the floor. Finally he raised his eyes to lock glances with his mother. "You know I do not."

"Then, I beg you will consider offering for my godchild, Anthea Heberdeen."

"Offering for her. I do not even believe we have met."

"No, you have not, but you will this evening. I want you to escort me to the Heberdeen Ball. Her brother, Sir Bertram, is giving it for her. God knows what put the idea into his mind. It is late to bring her out. She lacks but five months of being twenty. I tried to suggest that to him but he'd not heed me. He is utterly blind to her imperfections."

"Imperfections, Mother? Does she squint or . . ."

Lady Cornelia bit her lip. "I meant only that the child's a little shy and clumsy. Though she is well-looking, she is not an absolute beauty."

"You make her sound infinitely fascinating."

"No, I'd not call her . . . fascinating, but she has a sweet nature, she's sensible, and her dowry is well enough if not princely. Furthermore," Lady Cornelia paused significantly, "she had two brothers—the eldest, Sir Anthony, was killed at Vitoria. The family runs to boys, on both sides. Anthea is the only girl of her generation. Her father had five brothers and only two sisters. Her mother had three brothers." Lady Cornelia fastened a stern eye on her son. "You must accompany me to that ball—for Vane, if for no other reason."

He appeared to consider the matter, then he shook his head. "I have an engagement I cannot break."

"With one of your opera dancers, no doubt?"

"I think that does not concern you."

"Titus," Lady Cornelia put a compelling hand on his arm, "might I remind you that since the time of Henry IV, Vane has passed from father to son in one long unbroken line?"

He moved away from her. "I am not ready . . ."

"You will never be ready. I do not ask that you forget the past. For God's sake, Titus, come and meet her, at least. I do not say that you must offer for her, but I do say this: She is a pleasant, biddable young woman. She would make a good impression on the county, she would be a good mother to your children, and she would make no demands on you. And she is a Heberdeen."

"From all you say about her, she has every chance of remaining one," he retorted caustically. "And mind you, if I do decide to accompany you to the ball that does not mean I have committed myself in any way. You do understand that."

If Lady Cornelia felt a great surge of hope at this grudging concession, she was wise enough not to express it. With unwonted humility she said, "Thank you, Titus. I quite understand."

When the door had closed upon his parent, Titus moved to the mantlepiece and looked at the portrait for a long moment. Then he put a finger to that painted visage and drew his hand back as quickly as if he had been stung.

"Guilia, *cara*," he said brokenly and flinging himself into a chair, he buried his face in his hands.

It was almost time for her to join her brother, and Anthea, sitting at her dressing table with Debbie, her maid, putting the final touches to her coiffure, regarded herself in her silver hand mirror.

"Oh, miss," Debbie moved back. "If you ain't a sight."

"Um, that's exactly how I should describe it myself," Anthea remarked dryly. Meeting the maid's puzzled stare, she did not elucidate. Debbie had never seen her mother, so she could not know how ravishing the late Lady Heberdeen had looked in the diamond tiara. Anthea could not like it in her own hair—it needed her mother's pale locks to set off its silvery glitter. The gown pleased her no more than it had earlier in the day and it seemed to her that her blue eyes, framed by their dark brown lashes, were too staring while her color was too high.

A timid knock aroused her from her moody reflections. "My dear," a hesitant voice murmured. "Might one come in?"

Anthea summoned a smile. It would not do for Cousin Matilda to find her in the dismals. It would occasion a host of probing queries from the lady—most of them centering on the workings of her stomach, that organ being a favorite topic of her elderly relative. "Pray do come in, Cousin," she called.

"Ah, my dear." Miss Matilda Lawler, thin, gray of skin and hair, bore little resemblance to Lady Sophia Heberdeen, who had been her first cousin. She had elected to wear a gown of gray silk which made her look almost ghostly, especially since she seemed to drift rather than walk across the floor. Stopping a few paces away from Anthea, she clasped her long narrow hands together and exclaimed, "Ah, lovely, lovely, I do wish dear Cousin Sophia were here to

see you. How pleased she would have been. Such a becoming gown."

"Do you think so? I should have preferred a color to
white."

"No, no, no." Cousin Matilda followed each negative
with a shake of her head. "White is the only suitable color
for a young girl."

"But I am not a young girl." Anthea's smile was eclipsed
by annoyance.

"One would not call you old, child. Such nonsense as
runs through that pretty head. I become quite out of patience
with you. And I beg you will smile when you descend the
stairs. I should not like dearest Bertie to see you gloomy.
I hope you are not feeling queasy. I have just the rem-
edy . . ."

"Please no. Bertie's already dressed, then?"

"And has been this last hour. The dear boy looks so
handsome." Miss Matilda heaved a sigh. "Ah, I can remember when he waltzed . . ."

"I pray you will not, Cousin," Anthea cut in. She rose.
"You are finished with me, Debbie?"

"Oh, yes, miss, and you look a picture."

Anthea's dormant sense of humor stirred and almost
prompted her to demand "of what?" However, mindful of
her cousin, she suppressed the impulse and thanking her
maid, she came out into the hall and descended the winding
stairs to similar praise from her brother, who smiled up at
her from below. Looking at his handsome face, topped by
waving locks which were precisely the same silvery gold
as those of their late mother, Anthea was hard put not to
duplicate her cousin's sighs.

Yet it was not a night for vain regrets. The musicians
had arrived and she could hear them tuning up their
instruments. The footmen were brave in scarlet and gold
livery, their heads covered by powdered wigs, and glittering
paste buckles on their shining black shoes. Robert, the
butler, had never looked more imposing in a suit that

seemed to be mostly gold. Candles were set in sconces all along the corridor. She had the fancy that the house, so long closed and shuttered, breathed again. It behooved her to swallow any qualms she cherished concerning her own success.

Though certainly he would have vehemently disagreed with her, she did not consider it her evening, but rather the private property of her brother, ready now to take his place in the Polite World. She smiled at him. "How grand Robert looks," she murmured and for a moment her mobile features reflected the butler's haughty and condescending expression, causing Sir Bertram to hastily clap a hand to his mouth and still his merriment.

Miss Matilda stared at Anthea with some alarm. She had never believed her talent for mimicry to be quite respectable, nor had she approved the expressiveness with which she could read aloud. It brought to mind that old tale of Dillys Heberdeen, Anthea's aunt, who had fled her home for the love of an actor. Miss Matilda did not know the whole of the story for it was never mentioned, but she rather thought the erring lady was conveniently dead. But she should not be thinking on old scandals at such a moment nor would she chide Anthea as she had on other occasions. It would not be in order, not with dear Bertie looking so happy and so very well in his dark blue satin evening clothes. Such a pity that one of his breeches must needs be pinned up—with his other leg so shapely in its silk stocking and the shining leather pump upon his slender foot. Silly to have tears in her eyes.

The brother and sister were a fine-looking pair and if Anthea were a mite too plump, surely the gentlemen must see that she had a lovely complexion and no need of a rouge pot to add color to her cheeks. Her blue eyes, slightly slanted and framed by those long, unexpectedly dark lashes, were quite her best feature. If the gown were not quite right, still the child was well enough, and with a portion which was adequate, she could make a good if not a brilliant match. It would be a pity if something positive did not result from this evening and Anthea, once she got over her initial shyness, could be charming. If only the gentlemen had the discernment to see beyond that . . . but now was not the time to dwell on such matters either.

It was like the hush before the storm, Anthea thought. The footmen, Robert, herself, Bertie, Cousin Matilda, even the very furniture in the hall seemed in readiness—and someone must arrive soon for it was time. She should have liked to have hurried into the drawing room to look out the window for then she would see if there were a cluster of carriages in front of the house. That was how it had been when her parents had given their balls and she, peering from the third-floor window, had seen the post chaises, the hackneys, the curricles, and the phaetons all pressed together so that the street was impassable and the horses neighing and the coachmen attempting to drive through, all the while cursing colorfully.

Robert cleared his throat and Anthea snapped to attention. She smiled at Bertie as the butler announced in his deep vibrant tones, "Lord and Lady Ramsey, the Honorable Miss Dorcas Ramsey."

Thoughts and shreds of thoughts sped through Anthea's mind as Lady Ramsey, dark like her daughter and clad in a cherry-colored silk, appeared on her husband's arm, with Dorcas, looking lovely in a blue that matched her eyes, at their side. She forced herself to smile at the trio, but Miss Dorcas Ramsey did not smile back at Anthea—her gaze was hard and accusing as it flicked over her face—but on turning toward Sir Bertram, it softened miraculously. Putting her little hand on his arm, she said falteringly, "My love, my dear love, at last we meet. If you but knew what it means to me to be allowed to see you once more."

"Dorcas," Sir Bertram exclaimed huskily and quite as if there were only the two of them present, he bent down to kiss her.

After that, everything seemed an anticlimax. Anthea was almost as dazed as her brother. As she greeted other arrivals, she smiled mechanically, while she tried to fathom the meaning of Dorcas's hard looks. Yet it did not matter what the girl thought about her, she decided. Bertie was looking wonderfully happy, and she was quite sure that if anyone were bespoken that night, it must be Dorcas Ramsey.

Anthea's feet ached. She had been asked to dance by numerous gentlemen, some of whom were Bertie's brother officers and who, she suspected, had asked her out of duty. She had also gone down a country dance with a young curate and waltzed with another gentlemen whose name escaped her. None of her partners had made any real impression on her—neither in looks nor conversation. Many of them had said much the same thing and that had pleased her, for she had not been required to invent new answers. Half the time she had merely smiled and nodded. Scanning the dance floor, it occurred to her that there being no new arrivals, she might not be asked to dance again for the rest of the evening—which would suit her. But even as this thought or, rather, prayer, crossed her mind, she saw her godmother purposefully making her way in her direction. Probably the son she had mentioned as "expected later," had finally put in an appearance. Cravenly she backed toward the entrance of the ballroom. Fortunately it was only a few feet behind her, and gaining the hall, she hurried to the library. Slipping inside, she quietly closed the door behind her and stood against it, a hand pressed to her heaving bosom.

"Ah, hah, what dragon's pursuing you, fair maiden?" demanded a pleasant masculine voice from somewhere beyond the radius of light cast by the two candles burning on the mantelshelf.

Anthea jumped. "No dragon," she panted. "Merely my godmother."

"Oh, is she so fearsome, then?"

"Not at all. But she would ask me to dance, you see."

"How very unusual of her."

Anthea could not restrain a giggle. "I am speaking about her son." In Lady Cornelia's commanding voice, she intoned, "Very soon, my son Titus will be joining me. I am most anxious that you should meet. You will find him an excellent dancer and I am sure your steps must suit."

Emitting a crack of laughter, a tall shadowy form arose from the Queen Anne chair. "Ah, it is she to the very life."

Anthea's cheeks burned. "You'll never tell me that you are acquainted with her!" she exclaimed.

"Tolerably well," he admitted, "but tell me—why do you harbor such a prejudice against dancing with 'my son Titus'?"

"My feet hurt," she said candidly. "If he had arrived earlier, I expect I must have done so, but our steps would not have suited. I am *not* an excellent dancer."

"You have other far more engaging talents."

"Alas, I should not have displayed them. My Cousin Matilda would have been most displeased with me."

"I am glad we are denied the lady's company."

"So am I, actually. By now she would probably be dwelling on her stomach at great length—and it is tedious."

"The good Lord preserve us from tales of tedious stomachs."

"Dear! I am afraid I do not sound very sympathetic."

"You sound delightful. You make it worthwhile, my coming."

"You speak as if you might not have wanted to come."

"If any such outrageous notion crossed my mind, I am glad it did not hinder me from arriving." He moved closer to her and the candlelight reaching his face brought a gasp from Anthea. "What is the matter?" he inquired. "Have I frightened you?"

"No," she assured him hastily. He was looking at her

questioningly, but she could not explain that, on seeing him clearly, she had experienced a most peculiar sensation. It had seemed to her as if her heart had skipped a beat and, subsequently separating itself from its moorings, had soared into her throat as she had beheld what was surely the most handsome young man she had ever seen.

"I am glad," he began and paused, for the door was showing signs of being opened again. Stepping quickly to one side, Anthea was just in time to avoid Lady Cornelia's precipitate entrance. She came to a dead stop glaring at the gentleman in front of her.

"I little thought to find you *here*! Might I inquire as to why you are not in the ballroom?" she demanded in those accents duplicated so aptly by Anthea.

"I have heard that Sir Bertram owned some rare editions and I am happy to say that I have discovered one," his laughing eyes rested on Anthea's face.

"You are pleased to jest with me, Titus, and I must tell . . ."

"Titus!" Anthea cried.

Lady Cornelia whirled, her frown vanishing. "My dear," she said effusively, "I was told you were here but . . ."

Anthea barely heard her. "You are . . . ," she began and paused, swallowing convulsively.

"Exactly, Miss Heberdeen. I am 'my son Titus.' I beg your pardon for not providing an immediate introduction but I cannot say I am sorry for it."

"Oh, dear." Anthea, not knowing quite where to look kept her gaze upon the floor.

Lady Cornelia, obviously in a state of confusion, said, "You . . . have not been . . . introduced?"

"We have now, Mother," her son returned. His amused glance rested on Anthea's flustered face. "My dear Miss Heberdeen, I would not dare ask you to dance—but I pray you will allow me to wait upon you tomorrow morning— and perhaps you will come driving with me? I promise you'll not need to do anything except sit."

It had been entirely reprehensible of him not to have identified himself at once—and certainly she should have chided him for this oversight, but the only words that came to her tongue were, "I should be delighted, my lord."

2

DILLYS PLAYFAIRE, CALLED Dolly both professionally and
by her friends, owned a snug cottage in the village of Islington. Located on Duncan Terrace, it consisted of a drawing room, a parlor, a small dining room, kitchen, and servants quarters below and three small bedrooms above. The
whole was cluttered with such furniture as had caught its
owner's eye in the towns she had played during her twenty
years as an actress. There were numerous knickknacks,
some of fine bone china, ivory, and crystal. Other items
were valued only for sentiment's sake and most of these
were to be found on the mantelshelf and table tops in her
windowed parlor, where she received her more intimate
friends.

It was to the parlor that she welcomed her niece Anthea,
having sent her abigail to the kitchen to partake of tea and

cakes with Mrs. Pitter, her dresser, who acted both as cook and personal maid. Indicating the gilt armchair with the lion feet in which Anthea generally sat, she moved to her chaise longue which, in common with the chair, was an example of the Egyptian craze which had swept England a decade earlier. The chaise, which most of Dolly's friends did not hesitate to pronounce atrocious, boasted a long gold crocodile which stretched its length along the cushioned green-satin back. Its head reared out of the armrest and its tail curled at the other end. Its feet were scaled and presumably crocodilian in execution. Its owner laughed at it and loved it. Sitting down on this monstrosity, Dolly Playfaire regarded her niece out of bright, interested eyes.

Returning her aunt's glance, Anthea thought, as always, how pretty she was with her red-gold locks, sparkling green eyes, and porcelain white complexion. Though she knew her to be close to forty, she could easily pass for ten years younger. Indeed, thinking of her father's other sister, her late Aunt Harriet, it was hard to believe that Dolly came of the same parents. Born fifteen years after her sister and six years after her youngest brother, she had not been welcomed by her parents. Her siblings had been of a like disposition, regarding the advent of an infant as a considerable inconvenience. She had been a lonely child, burying herself in books and spending most of her time in her schoolroom with Miss Moffatt, her governess, who, due to her brother being an actor, cherished a secret passion for the theater.

It was one she was able to indulge by the simple expedient of telling her employers she was taking her young charge on edifying excursions around the city. That these excursions were to Drury Lane, Covent Garden, and other less well-known theatrical attractions and that Miss Moffatt and Dillys often sat in the wings to watch Adrian Moffatt perform, was known only to the two of them.

Since Dillys's meals were taken in the schoolroom, no one but the servants knew how late some of these repasts were. Miss Moffatt was popular and not "above 'erself" as many of her kind could be, and no one ever sought to curry favor with Milady by informing on her. Consequently Miss Dillys Heberdeen, who had become as devoted to the theater as her governess, was sitting in the wings on the night when one Michael Playfaire, lately arrived from Dublin, astounded London as Romeo. It was family legend that he had come forth from Juliet's tomb to find and comfort a weeping Dillys and to assure her that he was not dead. In the process, love had blossomed between them. It had been followed by an elopement to Gretna Green and fourteen years of ecstatic happiness until Michael contracted a fever and died.

His widow had been inconsolable but, fortunately for her, she had been unable to indulge her grief. She was playing Lady Teazle in *The School for Scandal* in Bath and contracted to appear as Peggy in *The Country Girl*, David Garrick's adaptation of William Wycherly's *Country Wife*, the following week and so it had gone on for the ensuing six seasons. And it showed every indication of continuing, for Mrs. Playfaire, now easing into older parts, was well liked in London and the provinces. Indeed her longest periods of rest came only in the summer when the weather was too warm to attract audiences to the largely airless and overheated theaters.

Now with her eyes fixed on Anthea's face, Dolly said, "Something momentous has taken place, else you would have presented yourself here a fortnight ago."

Her niece flushed and nodded, " 'Tis true. I have wanted to get away but 'twas not possible. Indeed I'd planned to come here the day after the ball but . . ."

"Child," Dolly interrupted impatiently, "I beg you'll not weary me with prologues, I never could abide 'em, nor epilogues, neither. What has happened?"

"Bertie's betrothed," Anthea said with a tiny sigh.

"Ah, when did that happen?"

"The night of the ball."

"Your ball?"

"Mine," Anthea said wryly.

"But . . . how could it take place so soon? You'll never be telling me it was love at first sight!"

"No, 'twas Dorcas Ramsey."

"Dorcas Ramsey?" Dolly frowned. "Not the chit who left him so severely alone all through his long illness?"

"She vows she was ill herself. She has told him that she went into a decline upon receipt of his letter and her parents were obliged to bear her to Brighton—where she lay for weeks in a coma. She swore she would go into yet another decline if he did not promise they would wed as soon as the nuptials might be arranged."

"Indeed?" Dolly's smile was mocking. "I think I should tell this tale to one of our aspiring playwrights. 'Twould make a capital romance and have the audiences in tears. However, if it is true, I am happy for Bertie. I am sure he must be happy."

"Exceedingly."

"And you, my love, what do you think? It seems to me that you were never fond of Dorcas."

Anthea sighed. "If she can make Bertie happy . . . it's all that matters."

"A noble sentiment. And so you and he are to be parted and all because of a ball he gave for you. Well, it has served one purpose—what about the other?"

Anthea studied her hands. "I vow I am in a quandary. It happened in such an odd way—and though we still laugh together, I feel a withdrawal at times as if . . . but I do not understand, though perhaps I refine upon it too much. I've not been acquainted with many gentlemen. Last week I saw him four times—he promised to come a fifth day, but he did not. However, he sent a note excusing himself and accompanied it with a great bouquet of red roses. I did not expect to see him after that, but I did the following Monday—and again he promised to come on Tuesday but did not arrive until Friday—and was off on Saturday to his home in the country and returned yesterday. He wanted to see me today, but I put him off because I had made up my mind that I must come to see you."

"My dear, I am sure that you are positive you are making excellent sense, but who, pray, is *he*?"

"Oh, did I not tell you?" Anthea blushed. "His name is Titus Croydon. He's the younger son of Lady Cornelia Croydon but his brother, alas, was killed, and so he is the Earl of Vane. Lady Cornelia is my godmother."

"Yes, I heard that Sophia had chosen her . . . I did not understand it at the time. She was ever full of her own consequence. I knew her well when I was young. She was a friend of my sister Harriet. I expect she's not changed a particle."

"I expect not. She is very proud and, I think, much used to having her own way."

"And is this Titus equally autocratic?"

"No, at least he does not seem to be. There's a strong physical resemblance between them—but he must favor his father as well. He is . . . very handsome." Anthea stared at her hands once more, aware that she was blushing again.

"Ah . . . but handsome is as handsome does. You seem to like him."

"Yes."

"And you said, also, that you still laugh together. What does that mean?" She listened carefully as Anthea detailed the circumstances attendant upon her meeting with Titus Croyden, laughing herself as the account ended. "But that is delightful. He must have been enchanted. I could wish for no better introduction to you, my dear. You were at your best. And he has pursued you since, it seems?"

"I have seen quite a bit of him, but I cannot help but think he does not like me as much as he did at first."

"Does not like you?" Dolly echoed incredulously. "But you've just told me you've seen him at least four times in one week, twice in another, and should have seen him today. I'd say that indicated a seriousness of purpose."

"Oh, I pray you'll not say so, Aunt," Anthea protested.

"Are you tiring of him, then?"

"Oh, no, I never, never could . . . but you see, he is so much more than I ever expected. He is handsome, charming, a friend of the Prince Regent, and welcomed everywhere. When he has taken me driving in Hyde Park, so many beautiful females seem to have an acquaintance with him, and each time I could see they were surprised that he was with me."

"Jealous, more likely."

"I am sure they were not," Anthea said earnestly. "Indeed, why should they be? I am not beautiful. I am shy and awkward."

"Not with him, obviously."

"Not with him, no, but certainly I am unlike the women he has known."

"Perhaps that is all to the good," Dolly said sagely. "And you do disparage yourself too much, my love. You are beautiful . . ."

"I am far too plump."

"No wonder, being shut up in the house with your brother, tending him night and day and hardly ever getting out for a bit of exercise. But enough of that. Despite what you say, this Titus Croydon seems to have been living very close to your pocket. Child, I know you are not worldly, but sure you must be aware of that."

"I—I am." Anthea faltered.

"Then?"

"I do not understand it." She fixed grave eyes on Dolly's face. "Pray do not let your liking for me influence your judgment, Aunt. Should you think that a gentleman of the first rank—a Corinthian—would find me beguiling, who has practically no knowledge of the Polite World? Indeed I have been quite tongue-tied when he has introduced me to acquaintances in the park and once, when he was assisting me from his curricle, my feet got tangled in my skirts and had he not caught me, I should have fallen flat. I could see by his expression that he thought me very clumsy."

"I am sure that is your imagination. He has continued to call."

"It happened the fourth day I was with him and as I told you, he sent his excuses on the fifth day."

"They had probably nothing to do with your descent from his curricle. Now hear me, my dear. You have birth and breeding. You are intelligent and kind. That is apparent to anyone who's been in your company upward of five minutes. The qualities you possess are enduring. Indeed I am of the opinion that any gentleman who won you for his wife would be more than fortunate. Do you believe he might offer for you?"

"I . . . his mama has hinted at it and surely, if he were not interested, he'd not be quite so attentive. Even Bertie, who is much concerned with his own affairs these days, has commented upon it. He did seem surprised when I told him I could not drive with him today."

"It was very brave of you, my child, particularly when you must have longed to accept his invitation."

"I wanted to see you. I'd put it off far too long."

"You are a dear girl and I think you may have your reward. It's good strategy to keep a gentleman on tenterhooks."

"I cannot imagine that he's ever been on tenterhooks. If you were to meet him, I am sure you'd agree with me."

" 'Even so quickly may one catch the plague,' said love-smitten Olivia," Dolly smiled. "And you are truly plague-struck, I fear." Her eyes narrowed. "Enough to contenance Lady Cornelia as a mama-in-law?"

Anthea flushed up to the roots of her hair. "I cannot believe it will happen. He is so far above . . ."

"Hold," Dolly raised an imperious hand. "I pray you'll not say another word on that subject, and I adjure you to banish it from your mind. If he should offer for you, you must not convince yourself that he is getting the worst of the bargain. It is no way to begin a marriage. If you've even a doubt as to the nature of his affections, I beg you'll think twice before you give him your answer."

"Oh, Aunt, it will not come to that." Anthea rose and took a turn around the room, inadvertently bumping into a table. She caught a china dog before it tumbled to the floor and said, "You see."

"I see that this room is as cluttered as a shop. Love, don't suffer so."

"Oh, dear." Anthea shook herself, continuing resolutely, "I have prattled far too long about my concerns. Tell me about your plans for next season. You'll soon be ready to go on tour, will you not?"

"In September," Dolly regarded Anthea anxiously, wishing she did not agree that a shy, unworldly and, alas, awkward female like her adored niece had little chance of bringing down a fashionable young buck such as she had described, unless he had some ulterior motive. That did not seem possible in the case of Titus Croydon, the wealthy and eminently eligible Earl of Vane.

At that same moment Lady Cornelia, plagued by similar doubts, sat in her son's parlor, drumming impatient fingers on the arm of her chair. A sound in the hall alerted her to his return, and shortly he joined her, looking tired and not at all welcoming. He was still in evening dress and a faint but heady perfume assailed her nostrils. It was not a scent he affected but, as a woman of the world, she forebore to comment on it, particularly since she had detected a look of ironic amusement in his eyes as he said, "Good morning, Mother, I hope you've not been waiting long."

"It's of no consequence," she replied shortly.

"As I've told you before, it's best to give me warning before these—er, visits."

"Yesterday, you told me you intended to take Anthea Heberdeen driving in the park." Lady Cornelia struggled against temptation but could not restrain herself from inquiring, "Why did you change your mind?"

"I did not change my mind, Mother. The invitation was rejected."

"Rejected!" she echoed incredulously. "Surely you are jesting!"

"Alas no, the lady informed me that she had made other plans."

"What other plans?"

"She did not elucidate!"

"I find that upsetting."

"I suggest you do not trouble your mind about it. The bird's in hand. It wants only the right word and 'twill be caged."

Her eyes narrowed. "And will you say that word?"

"Last night I bade farewell to Elise."

"That's no answer."

"I am sure I'll not shock you when I tell you that Elise was my mistress. It is customary, Mother, when a man's about to wed, that he rid himself of all encumberances—at least for the nonce."

His mother's eyes gleamed. "You will marry her, then?"

"I shall."

"Oh, Titus," Lady Cornelia's hard eyes actually filled with tears. "I do thank you."

"No need to thank me, Mother. On the contrary, it's I must thank you for finding Anthea Heberdeen."

"T-thank me?" she gasped. "Are you telling me that you love her?"

He shook his head and his dark eyes grew somber. "I am not telling you that, because though I wish I could, I do not, but I like her. Indeed I like her so much that I am not at all sure I am not doing her a great disservice by wedding her."

"I—I do not understand you," she said confusedly.

"She is the most delightful creature . . . or can be, when she is at ease. It seems she deserves something better from the matrimonial mart—but I tell myself that none will ap-

preciate her quite as much as I. And since an heir is desir-
able . . ."

"It's been five years," Lady Cornelia began tentatively.

For a brief second his eyes were filled with raw pain and
then his lashes veiled them. "If it were five times five and
fifty added, time could not heal this wound," he said in a
low voice.

She was silent a moment. Once more she was tempted
to argue with him and give him the benefit of her wider
knowledge of grief, but since such words would only anger
him and avail her nothing, she said merely, "When will
you offer for her?"

"In another week. I do not want her to think me too
impulsive, else she might confuse me with one of those
impetuous and utterly unbelievable heroes to be found in
the circulating-library romances dear Rosalie reads."

Lady Cornelia's smile was tinctured with relief. "You'll
not regret it."

His smile was quizzical. "I only hope that she will not."

"If you are kind, she'll have no cause for complaint. I
am sure you mean to be kind."

"Of that you may be certain."

"Few brides can even be assured of that. I need hardly
remind you that in our society it's dowries that are prized
the most. She cannot accuse you of choosing her for that.
Consequently she will believe what is more comfortable for
her to believe." She patted his arm. "And meanwhile, my
dear, Vane remains in our possession."

They were putting Holland covers on the furniture and
already the drawing room had a shrouded, ghostly appearance. Anthea, regarding it from the doorway, felt chilled
by the conglomeration of white shapes in its shadowy
reaches, the draperies having been drawn against the hot
summer sun.

She had the feeling that in leaving her home, she was
deserting an old friend. In a sense this house, in which she

had spent so many more years than at the distant Corners, was a friend or rather a haven. It seemed strange to realize she would never dwell under its roof again. She quickly shrugged this premature homesickness away; she would soon be living in a far grander abode than this one—or The Corners. Vane with its Adams additions and a vista created by Capability Brown was considered one of the glories of the country. Yet is still was difficult to be separated from this house and from her brother. Everything had happened so quickly. In a mere month, bright new threads had been woven into the tapestry of their lives. It was almost as if they were no longer the same people they had been on the night of the ball.

Imperceptibly, no, not so imperceptibly, Bertie was becoming Dorcas Ramsey's bridegroom—just as she herself was changing into Titus Croydon's bride. No, it was different. She was not being forcibly separated from her brother by the jealousy and suspicion of her groom.

Dorcas had not said anything, but her attitude remained chillingly similar to that which she had exhibited upon the night of the ball. There was the same hardening of her eyes each time she faced Anthea, there was the edge to her tone whenever she addressed her, and certainly there was no mistaking the relief with which she had greeted what she obviously believed to be an astonishing offer of marriage. It was all too evident that she had feared that a spinster sister-in-law would be foisted upon her household for the remainder of her days. Perhaps it was only natural that a bride would resent all those who had held her betrothed's affections—just as a groom might feel a similar resentment toward those his wife had cherished.

Yet she was sure that Titus felt no such animosity toward Bertie. Indeed it was difficult to know just what he was thinking at any time. However, he had seemed uncommonly pleased when she had accepted his offer—but for all that he had not been very demonstrative. The memory of his lips brushing her cheek came back to her. That brief kiss had chilled rather than warmed her, but Cousin Matilda had assured her that his restraint was not only proper but exemplary conduct on the part of an affianced bridegroom. Poor Cousin Matilda.

Anthea was glad to stop pondering on the "exemplary behavior" of Titus Croydon for the nonce. Suffice to say that she did love him, had loved him ever since first meeting him in the library. She was really singularly favored by fortune. If she had not been betrothed, she might easily have been forced to reside in some backwater with "poor" Cousin Matilda—for never would she have intruded upon Bertie! As it was, her cousin, given an allowance by Bertie, was going to York to stay with an old friend and share her house. It occurred to her that dear Cousin Matilda might want to take some of the furnishings of her chamber. It has been something else she had meant to discuss with her brother. Impulsively she moved out of the drawing room. She had left him in the library and very probably he was still there.

He was still there, his papers spread in front of him on the desk, as they had been when she had left him—but with him was Dorcas, who had arrived betimes. She was perched on the library steps and looked lovely in a white muslin gown adorned with blue ribbons. She had been laughing when Anthea entered, but on seeing her, her expression hardened and the look she gave her sister-in-law-to-be was both pained and resentful.

"Ah, good morning, Anthea," she said. "I've been trying to persuade dearest Bertie not to work so hard—so much of the responsibilities of the household have fallen on his poor shoulders—at a time when surely he should not be so encumbered."

The implied criticism brought a sharp retort to Anthea's lips which, in the interests of peace, she banished. She had relinquished the running of the household to her brother only reluctantly and at his determined request that she allow him to be useful. Anthea half expected him to favor Dorcas with that explanation but he only frowned and said in no very welcoming tone, "Well, Anthea?"

"They are nearly finished covering the furniture," she improvised hurriedly. It was, she thought regretfully, no time to put forth a request that might seem to pile still more responsibilities upon him.

"Ah, very good," he responded with a smile for Dorcas. "You are most efficient, Anthea."

Though the assurance, which could also be taken for a defense of his sister, had come too late, Anthea merely smiled at him. "I'll leave you. I must see to what I will take with me."

As she came into her chamber and rang for Debbie, she found herself feeling singularly depressed. It was not only that Bertie's attitude had undergone so extraordinary a change, it was that she was uncomfortably positive that Dorcas could not make him happy. She held a strange fear that the girl's dislike of herself could have ramifications which might prove very unpleasant to them all. She tried to shrug that thought away. Mrs. Peterson, her one-time governess, would have laughed at her, accusing her of being fanciful as she had when Anthea had confided similar premonitions to her as a child. With a little twinge of fear, she recalled that many of those had proved accurate. She chided herself for being ridiculous. What harm could Dorcas possibly wreak when they were soon to be separated by leagues and leagues—and she married to Titus Croydon?

"Nothing," she said out loud. "I am absolutely determined to live happily ever after, like Briar Rose in the fairy tale." She suddenly shivered. It had taken Briar Rose a hundred years to achieve that happiness!

It had rained in the night but on August 1, which was her wedding day, Anthea awakened early and saw a reassuring band of pink upon the eastern horizon. The short trip to the church of St. Martin-in-the-Fields would be warmed with sunlight.

It had been decided that brother and sister, becoming betrothed at almost the same time, must naturally be wed upon the same day. Their respective partners being agreeable, plans had been made accordingly. The brother was also enlisted to give the sister away. Thinking of this last task, Anthea smiled wryly, imagining Bertie's relief at the thought of relinquishing her to her bridegroom. Through her window she saw a small shred of cloud and could compare it to the tiny patch of regret that did not mar but did touch upon the happiness of the day. She could not be entirely comfortable knowing that the separation from her brother would be mental as well as physical. She, who had been so sure that his affection for her matched that which she entertained for him, was no longer sure of it. It seemed very strange that Dorcas could have effected this change in so short a time. It reminded her of something Mrs. Peterson had once told her. "Nothing is immutable; everything is subject to change." The governess had spoken with a shade of some remembered bitterness. "The very mountains that look so solid are constantly changing—rocks are displaced, snows erode them, the roots of trees bore into them."

"And I am changing, too," Anthea murmured. A thrill of anticipation helped to disperse her momentary melancholy. In a few hours she would no longer be Miss Anthea Heberdeen; she would be the Countess of Vane—truly of Vane, for she and her husband would be traveling to that particular haven directly after the wedding reception. In a fortnight's time they would be embarking upon a trip to Italy aboard the *Guilia*, Titus's yacht, presently anchored in Portsmouth. Anthea would have preferred that they leave immediately upon this voyage, but Lady Cornelia had assured her that it was a family tradition that all honeymoons begin at Vane. It went back, she had explained proudly, to the time when the first Baron of Vane had swooped down upon a wedding party and abducted the bride-to-be from her enraged groom, imprisoning her in his Keep and even-

ually convincing the outraged lady that though she had
little choice in the matter, she had made by far the better
bargain.

The idea of this traditional homecoming was both exciting and daunting. It could not please her that her mother-
in-law would be in residence. That, too, was a tradition,
for it had been the Baron's mother who had helped convince
his purloined lady that she would not regret his bold action.

"*Tradition be damned*!" Anthea started. That sentiment
uttered in the deep chest tones that Dolly Playfaire generally
reserved for Lady Macbeth had resounded in her ear quite
as if she were still in her aunt's parlor, whence she had
repaired for a visit two days previously.

"The idea of not letting the pair of you go off alone,"
Dolly had stormed. "What manner of man are you marrying
that he must needs let his mama dictate to him! And do not
prate to me of 'tradition'! There is a time when tradition
must give way to ordinary human considerations. There,
my dearest, do not look so dismal." She had whirled from
her accustomed place on her crocodilian chaise to fling her
arms around her niece, holding her tightly, protectively, as
she had added, "I am sure she will leave you in peace. It
is just that I should think she'd have some perception . . . but
enough! It might please you to be at Vane. It's known to
be a most beautiful house and the gardens are famous!"

Vane. They would be arriving there by early evening,
for it lay in Berkshire near the village of Caversham, and
the gardens in question were known to stretch down to the
Thames. Though it had not been a castle since the days
when Cromwell's men had leveled its walls, it had risen
again during the Restoration and stood square and solid
with huge magnificent chambers. Upon its completion in
1675, its state rooms had been visited by Charles II. The
great four-poster upon which he had slept remained in the
bedchamber along with a tradition that the lady of the house
had shared it briefly with the Merry Monarch, which was
possibly why the Baron had been made an Earl—dukedoms

being at a premium by that time.

Anthea had not garnered this last bit of information from Titus. Her aunt had picked it up from some unknown source. When Titus talked of Vane, he did not dwell upon ancien scandals. He spoke of it lovingly, mentioning with some pride that the estate had remained in the immediate family since the days of that enterprising first Baron. His eyes had lingered speculatively upon her and though such thoughts were foreign to her, she had felt as though he were already anticipating an heir. She had had a vision of herself as a settled matron with several children playing about her. Oddly, though she had always adored children and had fully expected to have a large family of them, that being a Heberdeen tradition, she did not want a baby immediately. It was very strange of her, she knew. Most of her friends had married, settled down, and produced infants within one to two years. Then . . . was that all there was to life? She moved restlessly and wondered what else she might expect from it. Was she being foolish to want something more? She rather thought she was. But . . .

A little knock on the door brought a period to her reflections. "Yes, Debbie," she called, thinking it was early for the girl to bring her tea—but perhaps she, also, was too excited to sleep. But it was not Debbie who answered as the door swung open. "It's Bertie, my love. May I come in?"

"Of course, my dearest," she cried, sitting up immediately.

Her brother, clad in a long brocade robe, hobbled in and coming quickly to her bed, sat down near her, enfolding her in his arms. "My very sweetest," he said in moved tones. "I've been thinking I've been singularly remiss in my treatment of you."

She clung to him. "No, no, dear," she assured him. "I know that you and Dorcas . . ."

He sat back, looking at her remorsefully. "She has been

nkind and I have let it pass. You must not judge her too
arshly. She wanted to nurse me, dearest girl, and felt
xcluded, which was my fault and mine alone. If I'd not
hought the task unpleasant . . ."

Anthea put a gentle hand over his mouth. "Hush, my
ear love, I do understand," she assured him, thinking pri-
ately that Dorcas would have made a poor job of nursing
er brother, tears and sighs having no place in a sickroom.

"You will always understand and forgive," he was say-
ng. "It is in your nature to be magnanimous. But, Anthea,
verything has moved forward so rapidly that we've had
o time to talk. I wonder, are you completely happy with
his man?"

"Entirely," she replied, aware that it was a poor word
o encompass the ecstacy that filled her at the thought of
eing Titus's bride, even given the few qualms that had
ssailed her that morning.

"Ah," he answered on a note of relief, "then I shall be,
oo. I do adore you, Anthea, and I will never forget your
indness to me when I came home."

She smiled at him tenderly. "It's no task to be kind to
hose whom you love, dearest Bertie, and I do love you so
much."

"And I you." He put a gentle hand beneath her chin and
tilted her face toward him. "You are looking well this morn-
ng. You will make a most beautiful bride."

"And you a handsome groom." Brother and sister em-
braced again and he limped from the room, closing the door
softly behind him.

Tears flowed down Anthea's cheek, but they were not
tears of sorrow. She glanced out the window. The little
shred of cloud, now golden in the glowing light, remained,
but the cloud upon her happiness had vanished.

A goodly number of the *ton* was present at St. Martin-
in-the-Fields. There was a contingent of officers from the

Royal Horse Guards, Bertie's old regiment. Sir William
Welby, a comrade-in-arms, was acting as his best man and
Dorcas's three sisters were her bridesmaids. They were a
charmingly pretty girls ranging in age from fourteen to
seventeen and with Dorcas's glowing smile duplicated on
their faces. Indeed joy radiated from the whole party and
seeing the corresponding glow in her brother's eyes, Anthea
could not find it in her heart to resent his bride. It little
mattered what manner of wedge Dorcas had inserted between brother and sister if she could bring that expression
to a face which had been somber for the long months of his
recuperation.

Watching them plight their troth, everyone wept happily
and, in an amazingly short time, Bertie was at her side
again and she ready to take her place at the altar. Unlike
Dorcas, she had not enlisted attendants other than her
brother and her Cousin Matilda, who was acting as maid
of honor. Titus's hasty courtship had precluded the sum-
moning of her two best friends from the country—one lived
in Scotland and the other in Nottingham. She did not miss
them; she was not minded toward exchanging giggling con-
fidences with them as they had with her before their mar-
riages. The speculations in which they had indulged, she
thought, would have dimmed the beauty of the occasion.

Staring down the aisle, it seemed to her that a great
length of red carpet stretched between her and her destination. All manner of thoughts ran through her mind as she
began her slow progress toward the altar. She wished she
might have looked like Dorcas in her white gown—so slim
so fairylike. As usual she felt clumsy and overlarge. Her
qualms increased when finally, and in a much shorter time
than she had anticipated, she stood beside Titus and Sir
Francis Tarleton, his best man, whom she had met only
briefly. A side glance showed her that Titus was looking
grave, even somber, but certainly he was amazingly handsome in his wedding attire. His coat, claret in hue and of

superfine cloth, became him, and it seemed to her that his figure had never been better displayed than in his buff-colored breeches, white silk stockings, and black leather pumps. His cravat was intricately tied and the stiff points of his starched shirt seemed to emphasize the strength of his chin. In spite of her aunt's strictures on the subject, she wondered once again why he had chosen her as his bride and, as usual, she could find no really satisfactory explanation.

Listening to the minister's exhortation, Anthea was aware of numerous silken rustlings and sighings. She guessed that the feminine half of the congregation was straining to get a better look at the man who was becoming her husband and no doubt, she decided with an interior wince, wondering why.

The minister said, "Wilt thou Titus Athmore Croydon take Anthea Beatrix Heberdeen . . ."

His response was slow in coming and so low in the uttering as to be barely audible. Again Anthea was aware of noise in the church—whispered speculations, perhaps, but he had spoken and it was her turn. Alas, her voice rang out far too loudly. She had sounded, she knew, both eager and bold. But she had not meant it that way. She had been very nervous, very unsure. Would he realize that? What was he thinking? What had been the reason for his hesitation? Bertie had spoken out loud and clear. He had not hesitated a single second!

Finally the ceremony was at an end and she was caught in her husband's embrace. His kiss, though brief, stirred pulses she had not known she possessed. Then Lady Cornelia moved forward to embrace her tearfully and, as she came out of the church to stand near Bertie and Dorcas, she was surrounded by people whose faces she barely recognized but whose congratulatory chorus was loud in her ears. Someone addressed her as Lady Vane—that sounded very odd—but everything was odd, exciting, and wonderful

for Titus had slid an arm around her waist. Looking up at
him, she failed to catch his eye. He was saying something
to his best man, but that did not matter because at his touch
all her incipient doubts had miraculously vanished and she
felt invaded by a happiness she had never experienced before.

3

"THERE, YOUR LADYSHIP." Debbie, having brushed out Anthea's long hair, stepped back, her face reflected above that of her mistress in the gold-framed mirror that hung above her dressing table. She smiled. Her eyes were bright with excitement but her flow of chatter concerning the magnificence of the chamber with its silk-hung bed, its carved chairs and painted cabinets, its tapestries and portraits, had ceased for want of acknowledgment from Anthea. "May I wish your ladyship, a good night?" At a nod from Anthea, Debbie curtsied and departed.

Anthea breathed a sigh of relief. She had found the girl's presence oppressive; she would have found any presence oppressive at that moment. Moving to the window, she pulled back the heavy green velvet draperies and looked into impenetrable darkness. It was odd not to see the glow of the streetlamps on the square nor hear the rattle of drays and carriage harnesses that reached the occupants in London houses no matter what the hour. Here, the silence was equally impenetrable. No, not quite. She could hear the trees rustling in the breeze and a chorus of frogs and crickets. Looking up, her eyes found a slim young sliver of moon and masses of stars. Once she had known the shapes of constellations—she saw those same shapes now but had forgotten their names. Orion, Cassiopeia, Andromeda . . . she did remember those but had forgotten their shapes. She would need to ask Bertie. No, not Bertie, Titus . . . would Titus know . . . Titus. They had never talked of stars. What had they discussed? Dragons. They had not discussed dragons, either. It was only that his first words to her had concerned dragons. That disembodied voice in the shadowy library, that handsome stranger, whom she had wed so quickly that he remained a stranger and strange. Unwillingly she cast her mind back over the events immediately following the wedding ceremony.

Without being able to remember exactly how they had arrived, she could envision the two of them at the Ramsey mansion on Hanover Square, where the reception was being held. He had stood beside her smilingly acknowledging the good wishes and toasts of the wedding guests, but she had found the arm clamped about her waist oddly rigid, and, looking into his eyes, she had been chilled by a bleak, unfathomable stare.

They had been there less than an hour when he had suddenly said, almost brusquely, "It's time we left, if we're to reach Vane in the early evening." As an afterthought he had added, "Unless you'd like to remain a little longer."

"No," she had hastened to assure him. "I am ready to go."

She had been more than ready, she had been eager, for she was uncomfortably positive that more than one person present must have contrasted his chill demeanor with her brother's radiant happiness. She had hoped that once she

and Titus were alone in his post chaise, his odd mood would
pass, but they had not been together. Dolefully she wondered how many brides had embarked upon their wedding
journey in the company of their mothers-in-law?

"It is only in the most frigid weather that dear Titus will
travel in a post chaise or a coach. His brother was the same
and their father before them." That was Lady Cornelia explaining why Titus had chosen to ride outside, galloping
past the vehicle in a cloud of dust and returning to its side
only occasionally. Lady Cornelia had smiled as she had
proffered this explanation, but Anthea, more sensitive to
nuances than she had ever been before, noticed that her
smile did not reach her eyes and that her words had lacked
her usual conviction. She had concluded, "I pray you'll not
refine upon it too much, my dear." Then evidently forget-
ting that she had uttered this particular prayer, she had
repeated it two more times during the course of the journey.

Her glance fell from the sky to a silvery gleam between
the distant trees. She had not noticed it before, but knew
it to be the river. Astonishingly it was London's Thames—
no, London's possession no longer since it was flowing
through Berkshire or, more specifically at the end of those
famous gardens of Vane her aunt had mentioned. A memory
of Dolly's cluttered little parlor brought a wish to be there
instead of in this immense mansion, for which she was fast
developing an antipathy.

"No," she murmured. "I must be fair."

If she were to be fair, it was not Vane she disliked. She
knew she would have found the great hall with its chalk-
white baroque bas-reliefs of garlands, classical urns, and
portrait-busts of Grecian dieties affixed to a pale blue background, beautiful, had her husband been there to bear her
across the threshold. However, once she and Lady Cornelia
had alighted from the post chaise, Titus was not in evidence.
Instead she had accompanied her mother-in-law inside quite
as though she had been any arriving guest. Titus had entered
a few moments later with a smile and a graceful apology

concerning his tired and lathered steed. He had followed
it with an embrace, but, again, she had discovered no
warmth in it.

A neat housemaid had shown her to her chamber, and
later she had joined Lady Cornelia and Titus for supper in
a beautiful little room, hung with Chinese paper and furnished with authentic Chinese pieces which, Lady Cornelia
had explained, had been brought to Vane by an adventurous
great-uncle. She had duly admired them but she had not
been able to eat much. Under the eyes of her husband and
his mother, she had felt constrained, out of place, and,
oddly, as if her companions had been people she had met
for the first time, that very night.

Those feelings still persisted, and Debbie's sly glance
as she had helped Anthea change into a thin silken nightgown and a flowered peignoir, had served to augment them.
A short time ago the clock had chimed the quarter hour.
Titus had told her he would join her at ten. It must be near
ten—almost time for her to assume those wifely duties of
which her Cousin Matilda, looking very pink, had spoken
yesterday evening. "You . . . you will no d-doubt be surprised at . . . at certain, er . . . demands your husband will
make," she had stuttered. "While I am in ignorance as to
what these will entail . . . I . . . I've been told that they
are nothing out of the way when one is married."

Her Aunt Dolly had not stuttered but she had not been
much more specific, either. "You'll need to accustom yourself to a new intimacy, child. Lovemaking between a man
and his wife is not confined to chaste kisses upon the cheek.
It will be up to you to be . . . yielding, though, of course,
much of what will take place will depend upon the . . . wishes
of your bridegroom. I am sure that faced with your inex-
perience, he will be . . . considerate."

This peculiar confidence had confused Anthea, but at
her subsequent questions her aunt had flushed almost as
pink as Cousin Matilda and retorted crossly that she could
tell her no more than she had done already, save that such

experience, though it did not come all at once, was monstrous pleasant—if you were truly in love.

Love. She knew herself to be in love with Titus and she had thought—or at least she had hoped—that he, because of his hasty wooing . . . No, she had never been sure, and the events of the day had rendered her nervous and uncertain and . . . Without knowing why, for she had heard nothing, she turned and found him standing in the doorway.

He was wearing a long brocade robe and at his throat she saw the frill of his nightshirt. Since the chamber was lighted only by the candelabrum on the mantelpiece, his face was in shadow and she could not see his expression. A memory stirred. She thought of his shadowy shape rising out of the Queen Anne chair in the library on that night when she had found him to be "my son Titus." He had been charming. He had smiled. He had teased her. She had not seen that side of him this day, but they had not been alone together—not once, and now they were. She moved forward and stopped, feeling the pull of the drapery. She had been grasping it and had failed to let it go. Feeling foolish, she dropped it. The silence in the room was suddenly oppressive. She wanted to hear his voice. "Good evening, my lord," she said and was pleased that her interior tremors did not shake her tone.

"Good evening, Anthea," he replied and moved forward. Though he had seemed to take only a single step, another step brought him to her side. It was possible now for her to see the flames of the candles in his eyes and, miniaturized upon his pupils, her own face as in a dark mirror.

"'As in a glass . . . darkly,'" she murmured.

"I beg your pardon?"

"Your eyes," she said. "I expect you don't know what I mean . . . but I see my face in them."

"'For now we see through a glass, darkly; but then, face to face; now I know in part; but then I shall know even as I am known . . .' 'Twas Paul to the Corinthians, was it not?"

"Imagine your knowing it so well," she marveled. "I

have never quite understood that passage."

"Nor have I," he admitted.

"There was something about charity afterward," she said because she wanted to hear him speak more of that beautiful passage in his beautiful voice. She had not known it was so sonorous.

"'And now abideth faith, hope and charity, these three, but the greatest of these is charity.' That's easier to understand," he smiled. It was his library smile and she felt more at ease, though certainly it must be unusual to be reciting passages from the Bible at such a time. She wondered if he had an affinity for its words or for its message. Was he a deeply religious man? She did not know. She did not know anything about him. She sighed.

"Are you nervous?" he asked.

"No," she hesitated, then told the truth. "I expect I am."

"And I have done nothing this day to make you feel at ease. I am sorry for that."

His apology startled her. "I understand," she said.

His brows contracted. "What has my mother told you?"

She found the question puzzling, but answered, "She said you liked to ride outside the carriage."

"Oh. It's true."

"I do, too. You do not feel the motion when you're on a horse."

"Are you fond of riding?"

"Yes, though I've not done much of it lately. Bertie was so ill . . ."

"We'll ride here. And I will show you the park. It's most extensive."

"I should like to see it." She was feeling nervous again— nervous and expectant, though what she was expecting, she did not know.

"You are quite lovely. Your eyes are beautiful," he said. His voice had dropped several tones. His change of mood and subject startled her.

"It's kind of you to . . . tell me so."

He laughed. "A polite response . . . but not needful—and I am not being kind, but honest." He moved closer to her and caressed her cheek. His touch was light but it awakened pulses that sped through her body. She wanted to say something but shyness stayed her tongue. He was very close to her now—and of a sudden he gathered her gently in his arms and bore her to the bed, depositing her in its center. The swiftness, the unexpectedness of his action had deprived her of breath. She gazed at him wide-eyed, but could not see him very clearly. The curtains of the bed were blotting out the light from the candelabrum. His face was once more in semidarkness, his hands—his hands were at her throat, untying the ribbons of her peignoir. "We might have talked the night away . . . but 'tis better thus. I hope you are not frightened of me, Anthea."

"No . . . ," she said uncertainly.

"I think you are," he moved back from her. "I shall try to remember that . . . and be considerate, my dear."

He had used the very word employed by her aunt! She was amazed—and somehow chilled, though she did not know why—and then speculation fled. He was easing her peignoir from her shoulders. She flushed. Her nightgown was cut low across the breast. He would see . . . She bit down a little cry. His fingers had slipped into her bodice; lightly they caressed her breasts.

Surely her heart was beating at twice its natural rate and a pulse in her throat was beating, too, for he was pulling her gown down, as far as her waist. Stretching out on the bed and lying close beside her, his lips were brushing her throat and then she felt them at her nipples. A lock of his hair was trailing across her stomach. Her gown had been eased down further so that she was nearly naked—no entirely naked, now, for he had pulled it off.

She was glad of the darkness for she knew herself to be blushing furiously. Her face felt warm and grew warmer as she felt his hands stroking her thighs. Small moans escaped her. She could not suppress them and hoped he would not mistake them for fright. She was not frightened—or rather she was, but she was also excited. It was hard to separate the two sensations. It was hard to think at all, when his hands and lips were caressing her body. He moved away and she knew she did not want him to be away from her. She reached for him in the darkness and did not find him, but in another moment he was with her again. Touching him, she found him to be naked—and knew that was as it should be. She gasped, feeling his hand between her thighs, his fingers buried now in the soft curling hair that grew in that part of her body for which she had no name—that forbidden part which her nurses had warned her not to touch, lest some horrid doom befall her. Yet he was touching, reaching further, more deeply, stroking kneading until she felt herself on fire! Without her knowing how it had happened he was above her, the length of his body covering her, his thighs moving rhythmically against her. She clutched him as she felt a thrusting hardness where his fingers had been. It was followed by a dull pain. She moaned but not with pain. She was excited—she had never been so excited and as the thrusting increased in intensity, her excitement increased proportionately. His chest was rising and falling against her breast, he was panting as if he had been running and something was beating against her. It hurt, hurt, hurt . . . not enough to scream, yes, enough to scream at the tearing of a tender part of her and an invasion that joined her to him, locked her against his quivering thighs and held her while he pressed and then with a long sigh, sank down upon her, his lips against the hollow at the base of her throat and finally, he moved away from her to lie beside her, no longer touching.

She did not want him away from her. She craved that touching. Wanting to be closer, she dared to move nearer so that their bodies touched from hip to toe, dared to take his hand and hold it against her breast and kiss each finger, dared to whisper, "My love . . . oh, my love, my love . . ."

"Oh, God," he said. "Why . . . why did . . . why aren't

you..." He broke off, "I should not have...I did not think it would be . . . Oh, Christ have mercy on me." He moved from the bed and for a moment he was a shadowy shape in the darkness and then he was gone, the echoes of a slamming door reverberating in her ears.

Dolly Playfaire had not been wrong about the gardens of Vane. They were beautiful. Ranging around three sides of the house, they were actually three different gardens, divided from each other by low walls or clipped hedges. Those on the north were formal and patterned, those to the south grew in untrammeled wildness, but the stretch that ran down to the river was organized as to color. Broad strips of white, yellow, blue, pink, and purple flowers lay on either side of neat graveled paths. At odd intervals there were stone benches, and it was also possible to sit upon the low brick wall that fronted the river. From that location the sloping grounds were a particularly lovely sight but one that Anthea, leaning against that same wall, failed to appreciate.

It was her third day at Vane and she had not seen her husband since that first and what she was beginning to term "fatal night."

She had lain awake a long time after his departure, her body still quivering from his invasion but fear replacing her excitement as she puzzled over his words and wondered what she had done to displease him. It must have been what she had said, but she had only told him she loved him. Why should that have angered him? Had she been too bold? She continued to puzzle over it until sleep overtook her. She had awakened late in the morning and noticed that Debbie, coming to help her dress, had been much quieter than usual.

On coming downstairs, she had met Lady Cornelia in the hallway and had had the feeling that her mother-in-law had been waiting for her—for she had come forward hastily to take her by the arm and to say more gently than was her wont, "My child, Titus had to leave."

"Leave?" she had repeated blankly.

There had been a glint of anger in Lady Cornelia's eyes, but she had spoken soothingly. "A message from his man of business . . . something with the Funds. It was necessary to go at once to London. He'll be back soon, never fear. Meanwhile you'll have the opportunity to become acquainted with your new home. You must let me tell you about it. I will show you through it later this afternoon. Should you like that, my dear?"

Lady Cornelia had spoken so decisively that Anthea had had the feeling that she must agree whether she liked it or not. "Yes, of course," she had said in a small voice, only wanting to be away from the woman so that she might be by herself to think, but instead she had been bade to come to breakfast. She had not been able to eat. No more had been said about Titus's absence, not that day or the next, but, of course, she did not believe Lady Cornelia's explanation. She was miserably sure that it hinged upon what had taken place on their wedding night. Yet, despite this conviction, she had prayed and hoped for his return. Yesterday the sound of wheels on the driveway had brought her running from library to hall only to find the butler admitting a pretty, fair-haired young woman and two beautifully dressed little girls who looked much of an age. They had been followed by footmen bearing trunks and bandboxes. Meeting the new arrival's inquiring stare, Anthea had shyly told her, "I am Anthea Croydon."

"Anthea Croydon," the young woman had repeated with an edge of surprise to her tone. Then, after the barest of pauses, she had hurried to take her hand, "You must be Titus's bride. I am Rosalie Croydon, your sister-in-law, and you must meet Eva, and Edith, my girls."

As the two children had curtsied shyly, Lady Cornelia's robust tones had echoed through the hall, "Ah, Rosalie, you are returned early."

Rosalie had stiffened perceptibly, "Yes, my mother was not well and the children . . .," she began.

"I see," Lady Cornelia had joined them. "I am sorry to

hear that your mama is not well. I hope the ailment is of little moment."

"Her old complaint," Rosalie had explained. "Rest has been prescribed by her physician."

"I see," Lady Cornelia had repeated.

Even in the depths of her unhappiness, Anthea had not failed to realize that a sense of strain existed between the two women. She read disapproval in Lady Cornelia's eyes and thought she discerned a flicker of bitterness in Rosalie's gaze. She also noticed that the two little girls regarded their grandmother nervously, almost fearfully, while she had not even appeared to be aware of them. Given these undercurrents, Anthea had been extremely glad when, after a few moments of desultory chatter, the gathering had dispersed. Rosalie explained that she must unpack and speak to the children's governess, and Lady Cornelia invited Anthea to join her in the orangery. She had summoned up the courage to refuse, saying diffidently that she wished to rest.

She had not gone to her chamber, but had gone, instead, to the long gallery. That great hall, hung with family portraits, was furnished with comfortable chairs and couches. Through six lengthy windows, it was possible to see a segment of Capability Brown's vista. However, it was neither this view nor the generations of Vane portraits which had beckoned her there. It was a family group she had noticed on that painful first afternoon when Lady Cornelia had shepherded her through the house. The painting depicted a younger, pretty Lady Cornelia smiling proudly up at her two sons. The elder boy had been tall, grave, and proud of contenance, as if he already bore his illustrious title. Titus, however, looked much different. His head was thrown back, and he possessed a bright gleam of humor in his eyes and a singularly sweet smile. Charm and gaiety had radiated from him. Though she had had some acquaintance of his charm and humor, she realized that the gaiety was missing. In repose, his face was almost as grave as that of his late brother.

"What happened?" she had murmured to the boy in the portrait. "What changed you?"

The painted eyes had only gazed at something beyond her, something that had pleased him as she had not been able to do. She had gone quickly forth from the long gallery, her mind once more filled with the puzzling happenings of the first night. What could she have done to send him not only from her bed but from the house, the village, the county? She had found herself quite unable to face Rosalie's questioning glances; she had supped in her chamber that night and thought she had glimpsed a pitying look from the maidservant who had removed a tray full of largely untasted dishes. She wondered what the other servants must be saying about her, and about their master's hasty departure. It mattered little. All that signified, was that he had gone and that she remained alone and in torment.

"Oh, God," she murmured out loud. "What could I have done? What?" Burying her face in her hands, she burst into tears.

"My dear . . ." The voice, low and compassionate, startled her. She blinked up at a Rosalie haloed by a nimbus of tears. "Oh," she hastily drew a hand across her eyes. "I . . ."

"I should not intrude," Rosalie spoke gently, "but I know you must be sadly confused." She sat down beside Anthea and put an arm around her. "My maid told me that Titus left in the early morning." Her arm tightened and she drew Anthea closer into her embrace. "It is cruel . . . too cruel that all of us must suffer because of that woman."

"That . . . woman?"

"Lady Cornelia." Rosalie's eyes were full of indignation. "It is she you must blame for Titus's defection. Or blame me who produced daughters instead of sons. Poor mites, can you see how much she dislikes them?"

"Surely not . . .", Anthea began confusedly.

"Oh, yes, she does. Because they are not boys, you see. It was why I was brought into this family. I, the youngest of five children, three boys, two girls. Odo was ordered to offer for me and like a dutiful son, he did. Still I'd not thought she'd prevail so easily on Titus. They'd been so long estranged and there was Guilia and the child . . ."

"Guilia and . . . the child?"

Rosalie's hand flew to her mouth. "Oh, I did not mean . . . but I thought he must have told you. Oh, dear, he did not mention Guilia?"

"Who—is Guilia?" Anthea asked.

Rosalie looked distressed. "I should not tell you, if they did not, but you ought to know. It's only fair, rather than you blaming yourself for whatever took place between you." Meeting Anthea's startled glance, she added, "Believe me, I understand how you must be suffering. I've had my share of it. It's not easy to realize that you have been selected in much the same way a canny horse breeder selects a brood mare. I was a pretty girl. I had a good opinion of myself, and many suitors. I thought Odo wanted to wed me because he loved me, not because I had three brothers."

"Three . . . brothers?"

Rosalie nodded. "Yes . . . which suggested to Lady Cornelia that boys ran in my family and that there would be an heir at Vane. You see, the estate and title has descended in one unbroken line . . ."

"I know," Anthea interrupted. "Titus told me. But it can't be true that you, who are so lovely and . . ."

"I thank you, my dear, but it is true. Lady Cornelia, with only two sons, wanted both to breed as soon as possible." Rosalie laughed harshly. "I did not find that out until after the birth of my second daughter and heard Odo defending me, because by then he had become reconciled to the match and to me. If he had lived . . ." She sighed, and seemed lost in the past. "But he did not," she continued, "and in consequence, Titus was forgiven and welcomed back to Vane. I do not think he would have come were it not that he was despairing. And, in common with Vanes, he loves his home."

"What happened?" Anthea demanded. "Why was he despairing? Why did he need to be forgiven?"

"Because, my dear, he had done the unthinkable and the seemingly unpardonable. He had fallen in love with the daughter of his fencing master and, instead of making her his mistress, he had married her. I was not here at the time, but Odo told me of Lady Cornelia's reactions. She screamed down curses on his head and cut him off without a penny. I cannot think it worried him unduly. Guilia di Rossi. She was an Italian girl, very beautiful, and Odo told me, almost enviously, that they adored each other. Titus changed his name and went to work with his father-in-law as a fencing master. I expect that, title or no title, he'd have been there yet had not Guilia died giving birth to a son, who also died."

"Oh . . .," Anthea said pityingly. "How very tragic for him."

"Yes, tragic. It's been five years since she died and I'd not thought he'd marry . . . but I'd reckoned without Bartholomew's excesses and Lady Cornelia's powers of persuasion. Bartholomew is Titus's second cousin and the heir. He's a horrid little man who has a huge family of boys and girls. He lives on Lady Cornelia's bounty and what monies he does not gamble away, he converts into gin. I cannot blame my mother-in-law for not wishing to see him at Vane—and Titus also holds him in disgust. Have you brothers, my dear?"

"Two."

"And uncles?"

Though she was hardly in the mood for smiling, she could not restrain that expression as she replied, "My father had five brothers and my mother had three."

"Ah, then you must heed me." Rosalie turned compelling eyes on Anthea's face. "Do not be a fool. Give Titus his children and let us pray they are all boys. Then, insist you wish to live in London. Had I not been so foolishly in love with Odo, I should have done the same. Married females with indifferent husbands need not rusticate in the country.

They can drop their brats, leave them with wet nurses, and enjoy themselves in all manner of pleasant ways—as long as they're discreet. If you should need a companion, I beg you'll consider me. Only I pray you, Anthea, do not blame yourself for Titus's momentary defection. He'll be back. Having made this one great concession to his mother, he'll make another. She is a most persuasive woman. I see I have hurt you, but is it not better to know the truth than to dwell in an atmosphere of misery and doubt?"

Anthea jumped down from the wall. "Yes, it's much better," she agreed. "And I do thank you for telling me." Then, because she could not trust herself to say anything more, she ran up the slope toward the house.

"But 'tis monstrous!" Dolly Playfaire took a quick turn around the parlor and then came back to kneel beside Anthea, who sat bolt upright on her accustomed chair, her hands clasped so tightly together that her fingers had turned red and her knuckles white. Her face was also white and her eyes wide and staring. She wanted to brush the girl's tangled golden hair back, but knew that Anthea would consider that a pitying gesture. And the young woman did not want to be pitied. She was in a towering rage. Dolly said, "If you had waited until he came home . . ."

"I did not want to wait. I did not want to see him," Anthea contended, a flush high on her cheeks. "I never want to see him again."

"But, dear, they will say you deserted him. He can sue you for divorce. You'll have no redress," countered her aunt.

"I want him to sue me for divorce. I would start proceedings myself, were it not that it would mean seeing him again. I want to be free of him and I am sure he wants to be free of me."

"But, my poor love, have you considered the consequences . . . a divorced woman in our society." The thought seemed to shock even Aunt Dolly.

"I do not care a fig for 'our society.'"

"Your brother, what will he say?"

"He will say whatever Dorcas wishes him to say. She hates me."

"Oh, no."

"Yes, I tell you. And I do not care. Even if they were to beg me to come to them, I should not go." Anthea grasped the older woman's arm, and fixed her gaze upon her. "Oh, Aunt Dolly, I do not want to see anyone, I... I used to know. I pray you will let me come with you."

"With me?" Dolly amazed by the entire conversation, could not conceal her surprise at this request.

"Yes," Anthea said passionately. "There must be something I can do—be a prompter, sew costumes, help cue you in your roles—and mayhap in time I can even take small parts . . ."

"But, my dear," Dolly began perplexedly.

"You do not want me? Very well, perhaps I can find work as a governess or . . ."

"Nonsense, and it's not that I do not want you. Life in the theater's not easy. An actress, anyone associated with it, is not held in great esteem. Furthermore I wonder if you have thought your situation through. After all, you are the Countess of Vane and . . ."

"That means nothing to me."

"But if you'd stayed, perhaps . . ."

"I could not."

Dolly regarded her niece pityingly. In only a few days she looked much different. Evidently she had eaten very little, and certainly she could not have slept. She looked weary and disillusioned. Curse Lady Cornelia and double curse her wretched son. Together they had well-nigh ruined the girl's life. She doubted very much if Anthea would fit into the hectic round of the theater. She had only seen it from out front. She had no inkling of the work, the cold dressing rooms, the difficulty of obtaining proper lodgings at inns, where actors were considered in the light of thieves

and vagabonds, the dreadful traveling conditions which
sometimes necessitated their going on foot from town to
town if the coach broke down.

No matter, she could not tell her about these now. She
could not pile fresh miseries upon her head. She said, "Very
well, my dear. I shall take you with me. I only hope you
will not live to regret your decision."

Anthea threw her arms around her aunt. "I do thank
you," she said in a moved voice.

It was a good sign, Dolly thought, that she did not cry.

Part Two

4

LONG, WIDE, AND high of ceiling, the pump rooms at Bath were built to accommodate a great many people. Yet during the morning hours they always seemed filled beyond capacity. Beau Nash, that genial but strict and certainly snobbish Arbiter of Taste, who had had the ordering of them during the previous century, would have decried the numbers of honest but plain citizens who were there congregated to drink the acrid but eminently health-giving waters. Nor would he have been pleased to see so many of the *haut ton* mingling with their inferiors to lift a glassful of that restoring liquid.

The Beau had never championed democracy. He would have had other objections equally serious. He had been known to abhor gossip to the point of inserting a directive in that list of rules concerning good conduct that yet hung on the door. It read: "All repeaters of such lies and scandal must be shunned by all company." Needless to say, that and all the other rules were sadly ignored by the present generation. Indeed those who were not regaling their companions with a lengthy recital concerning their disturbed interior organs were most certainly discussing their fellow men or women, often in tones loud enough to pierce the babble.

Consequently a tall thin lady looked down her very prominent nose at a beautiful fair-haired girl fashionably garbed in a blue lute-string gown. She was talking to a tall, broadshouldered man, whose well-cut garments proclaimed him to be a patron of a fashionable tailor and whose handsome features drew more than one admiring feminine eye. However, the eye of that thin lady was far from admiring, as she remarked loudly, "But she's a play-actress and there's no doubt but that he's her Protector. It's a wonder he did not have the good grace to leave her in Avon Street—where such doxies belong."

"Shh, my dear Tabitha," cautioned a small man at her side. "Do you not know that he is the Marquis of Fearing?"

"Disgraceful," snapped the lady. "In my day noblemen did not parade such creatures in public places. I shudder to think what the Beau must have said."

"I know what I should like to say and immediately," muttered the Marquis of Fearing, his hazel-green eyes grown hard and his mouth compressed into a thin line.

"Lud," the girl at his side smiled gaily up at him, "I pray you'll not take umbrage, my lord. I am quite used to it and so is Aunt Dolly." She indicated her relative, currently quaffing the waters and making a dreadful face. "If," she continued, "you were to defend me to every one of my detractors, you should end the day sadly exercised about the tongue."

"It would be exercise in a good cause, my dear Miss Playfaire," he smiled.

"Oh, this water's vile," Dolly Playfaire shook her head

and set the glass down on an adjacent table. "I'll not drink another drop—no matter what it might do for me. I might add that I do not feel one whit better for having partaken of it."

"Its effects are cumulative, at least that is what I am told by the attendant," her niece said.

"Who doubtless wants you to come back each morning." The Marquis shot a look in the direction of the said attendant and was not surprised to find him looking in their direction.

Dolly turned to her niece and remarked, "I notice that you've not taken so much as a sip, Thea."

"Watching your expressions quite daunted me," she replied. "Though I think you should save 'em, Aunt, they would do credit to a Duchess of Malfi in her death throes."

"Quite right," commented the Marquis. "Poison, I see hath been thy timeless end."

"Faugh!" came a loud exclamation followed by a spurt of water that, judging from the outraged cries of several persons, had wetted them. A rotund gentleman was to be seen wiping his mouth with the back of his hand, and a moment later he was shouldering his way toward the door, growling, " 'Tisn't fit for pigs."

"Pigs," the Marquis repeated. "It seems to me that these waters were discovered by pigs, which having contracted leprosy from their swineherd, one exiled prince—Bladud by name—were healed of the disease by accidentally falling into the hot springs, whereupon their master followed suit and was similarly healed."

"Oh," Thea nodded. "I know that tale. Mrs. Peterson, my gov—" She broke off flushing.

"I vow," Dolly Playfaire said quickly, "it's monstrous close in here. Might we not leave?"

"Please," Thea breathed. "Do you mind, my lord?"

"Not at all." Accompanying the two women into the sunny street, the Marquis indicated his curricle, an elegant equipage, its door inscribed with his crest in gold. Moses, his small tiger, was perched on the high seat holding a matched pair of spirited chestnuts in check. "I hope I may take you for a drive?" he said.

"That must give rise to even more gossip," Thea smiled.

"But my invitation includes your aunt," countered the Marquis.

"In that case, I should love it. Should you not, Aunt Dolly?"

Receiving a compelling look from her niece, Mrs. Play-faire said obediently, "Yes, I should, too. I do thank you, my lord."

"Excellent. I'll drive you past the circus and up to the Royal Crescent. We might even go as far as Prior Park, unless you've seen it and would find another visit tedious."

"No," she replied. "We've had little chance to see anything of the town. I've needed to con my part, for Aunt Dolly assures me that half the audience will know it word for word and will not be above shouting corrections if I am in error. Indeed I confess myself to be all aquake at the thought of performing the role of Lydia Languish in Bath."

He laughed. "I do not believe it for an instant, Miss Playfaire, having seen your charming performances in Bristol and . . ."

Thea raised a hand. "My lord, you forget that Richard Brinsley Sheridan was raised if not born here, and that he set his *Rivals* in Bath."

"I cannot believe an actress of your caliber could be intimidated by the great man, even if he were seated in the house."

"You are too kind," she dimpled.

"I am not nearly as kind as I should like to be," he murmured, casting a quick and wary look in the direction of Mrs. Playfaire and finding that she had fortunately moved out of earshot.

He received a cool blue look. "If we are to continue friends, my lord . . . ," cautioned Thea.

"We must," he said ardently.

"Then . . ."

"Very well, I will respect your wishes and I think I must respect you for your stand—even though I cannot help hoping . . ."

"Aunt," Thea called, "I think it were better that we returned to our . . ."

"No," he interposed. "I am properly chastened. I pray you, Miss Playfaire . . ."

"Very well," she relented with a quelling look. "Only . . ."

"You wish to return to our lodgings, my dear?" Mrs. Playfaire had joined them.

"No, she wished only to tell you that we are ready to leave," the Marquis said firmly. "Come, let me hand you up." Purposefully he led her to the curricle and as he was intent on helping her to a seat, he missed the roguish wink that she directed at her niece.

It was close on two hours later that the Marquis brought his curricle to a stop outside a house on Queen's Square and handing his reins to his tiger, escorted his fair passengers to the door of their lodgings. Though he smilingly acknowledged Mrs. Playfaire's words of gratitude for a pleasant and instructive drive, his gaze lingered on her niece's face. "I shall be in a box directly over the stage," he murmured.

"I had thought the theater wholly subscribed," she said in some surprise. "However did you manage that, my lord?"

"I can arrange nearly everything I really want." he replied in a low voice. "Indeed, until I met you, I did not need to say 'nearly.'"

"How tedious for you, my lord. I cannot believe that so ordered a life can have been other than monotonous."

"It had its compensations, my dear Miss Playfaire," he bowed over her hand. "Until tonight."

"Until tonight," she agreed.

"I could wish that those words carried more weight."

"For myself, I pray only that tonight will be as light as
Mr. Sheridan intended it should be, else I fear he would
rise from his grave to haunt me."

"I would envy the ghost who haunted you; at least you'd
not be able to dismiss it so easily." Bowing a second time
and with another bow for Dolly Playfaire, he went back to
his curricle. He issued a curt command to his tiger, seized
the reins, and was off.

Once having reached their suite of rooms which over-
looked a small garden brave with spring flowers, Mrs. Playfaire sank into a chair and regarded her niece thoughtfully.
She had never seen her in such looks. She did not hesitate
to attribute the lovely color and the bright eyes to the stim-
ulation Thea derived from the Marquis's company.

It was a circumstance that surprised, pleased, and, at the
same time, alarmed her. In the two years since Anthea, or
Thea, as she was now known, had been with her—first as
prompter, then in small roles and, once her very genuine
talent was recognized, leading parts—she had devoted all
her time to perfecting her craft. The other actresses in the
Symonds Company had been amazed at her rapid rise. But
Dolly Playfaire had ascribed her success to a deep desire
to be Perdita or Ophelia or *The Country Girl*—or indeed
anyone but Anthea Croydon, Countess of Vane.

If she had not come with her, not had the stimulus of
the work, Dolly shuddered to think what might have happened. There was no doubt but that the girl had loved the
man who had married her for reasons which had nothing
to do with love. It was a pity, it was close to a tragedy that
he had felt it necessary to try and convey some semblance
of that tender feeling. Indeed the very thought of Titus
Croydon was enough to make her frown and wish him in
Hades. She could wish it even more at this precise moment
for, after a year of rejecting all the other gentlemen who
so eagerly pursued her, Thea was finally showing signs of
interest.

Though her aunt was definitely concerned about a situation which, under the circumstances, was fraught with problems, it did prove that Thea must have finally recovered from her affliction of the heart. Yet the experience had made its mark. That, Dolly decided, was just as well. If there was a diminishing of her endearing gentleness and of the compassion which had rendered her so vulnerable, she had acquired wisdom and, at twenty-one and a half, she was, at least in attitude, a woman of the world. She was not to be cajoled by soft words or languishing looks. If she had met Titus Croydon today, she would have seen through his subterfuge in a moment. The Marquis of Fearing had turned the full panoply of his famous charm upon her and still, after an acquaintance of five months, she was holding him at arm's length.

Dolly smiled. Such restraint must be a new experience for a man who had been the good friend and Protector of more than one member of their profession, ending his re-lationships as casually as they were begun and emerging with at least his heart whole. She guessed that he was puzzled and intrigued by a beauty who seemed made for love. Her looks had improved wonderfully in the past two years. She was slim enough to have been called an "ethereal presence" by a York critic writing of her Titania in a *Mid-summer-Night's Dream*. Her slimness had revealed high cheekbones and caused her eyes to seem much larger. Their slight slant was more apparent and indeed Dolly had, per-force, to agree with those who called her one of the most beautiful young actresses to be seen on the boards. She could imagine that when she made her debut as Rosalind at Drury Lane a fortnight hence, she would have the London scribes agreeing with their provincial brothers. She frowned. Though that debut was inevitable, she was concerned about it. Anthea was appearing only once, before fulfilling an en-gagement in Birmingham, but there was always the possibil-ity that her husband would be present. If that happened it was necessary to be prepared for the worst, an ugly scandal.

The only reason that such a confrontation had not taken

place already was because Thea had steadily refused to let the Earl know where she was or what she was doing. There had been no arguing with her. In her desire to drop from sight, she had not even informed her brother of her where-abouts—though she had been persuaded to send him a letter telling him she could no longer remain with her husband and was living in seclusion on the Continent. Though Dolly had argued that Bertie would be worried, her niece had only said, "I'll not disturb his felicity and I assure you, in time he will not even think of me."

"I cannot agree with you," Dolly had stated. "I think he will be most concerned about your welfare."

"Dorcas will reassure him," her niece had responded dryly.

"Why are you so sure she does not like you?"

"She prefers to believe it was I who kept Bertie from communicating with her during the earlier stages of his recovery—mainly because it was my hand that wrote the letter breaking off their engagement."

"But she must have been told that it was done at his dictation."

"She believes what she chooses to believe and perhaps she knows that I do not like her. I cannot think what she would say were I to apply to Bertie for help. Best let me be a sleeping dog and lying where he cannot rouse me."

Yet a confrontation with Bertie was, in Dolly's opinion, unavoidable. Even if he were not, as she knew, a devotee of the theater, he must come to see her eventually. She frowned slightly. In the last two years she had heard from her nephew only once and that on the eve of his marriage. She had wondered at that. Possibly he was, as Thea contended, too happy in his marriage to seek her out, or was he fearful that his wife would learn of his disgraceful family connection: She forebore to speculate. What Bertie thought was unimportant; what mattered was Thea's interest in the Marquis of Fearing. If she were truly inclined toward him, she ought to have her chance of happiness, but how might that be? She would not, could not, become his mistress and, out of loyalty to her family, she would never reveal her true identity—unless she were to do it accidentally. Dolly thought of her near mention of her governess—which, fortunately, he had not caught, but surely he must realize that she was not the general run of actress, that her manners were the result of breeding and heritage, not art and . . .

"Aunt . . . Aunt Dolly . . ."

"Yes?" Dolly blinked at Thea.

"I think you must have been dreaming though your eyes were open," Thea laughed.

"I was thinking."

"Oh?" Thea looked a little self-conscious. "It was a lovely drive, was it not? And Clive handles the ribbons well."

"Clive, is it?" Dolly gave her a long look.

Thea blushed. "He has begged me to use his name. It is one kindness in which I can see little harm."

"And you have given him leave to call you Thea?"

"We are friends and for all he knows, I am a mere actress," she said defensively.

"Um, when was this new camaraderie achieved?"

"When he alighted to show me around Sham Castle. You'd not come. He called me Thea and immediately apologized."

"You should have accepted it and let it go at that."

"I pray you'll not chide me."

"How may I not when I see the direction in which your inclinations are tending. It is more than a mere friendship to you, then?"

"No, and can never be, but I—do like him."

"That is understandable enough. He is very pleasant, though, as I have told you, he has had other and warmer friendships among the females in our profession."

"You know me well enough to be sure I'll not allow more than I have granted."

"You've said that you like him. Would you ever like

him enough to tell him the truth?"

"The truth?" Thea's eyes darkened. "Does he need to know it? Might I not enjoy his company a little longer?"

"Do you imagine you will forfeit it if he knows?"

"He'll believe me wicked and depraved—and being such will be angry that I ignored his solicitations."

"Nonsense, he'd never believe you wicked nor depraved."

"He has harsh words for the Marchioness of Doyle . . ."

"She ran off with her lover. That is why she is held in such contempt."

"And I went upon the stage. That is the same in the eyes of the *ton*."

"Perhaps, but I cannot think that Fearing would ever hold you in contempt. And talking of this, one day you must come to terms with your husband."

"I am sure he must have divorced me by now."

"Would you not be the better for knowing? If you were to write to him . . ."

"No!"

"You must one day."

Thea's eyes were suddenly full of tears. "Not yet," she told her aunt. "I must rest, else I shall be in no condition to appear tonight."

"I think you must still care for him," Dolly frowned.

Thea actually stamped her foot. "I do not. I *hate* him," she cried passionately and fled into her chamber, leaving her aunt to shake her head and raise her eyes to heaven. She then followed her niece's example and sought her own chamber for a rest and a review of her lines as Mrs. Malaprop, a role she was close, she thought dismally, to living in real life.

The applause in the small theater was deafening, but it had finally ended and it was time for intermission. However, one couple did not leave their box, but remained in their seats staring at each other incredulously. They had not

spoken since Miss Playfaire as Lydia Languish had bowed
to loud cheers and thunderous applause. The silence between them was finally broken as Lady Heberdeen said
accusingly, "I do believe you knew about this all along."

"Of a truth I did not," he responded, and then much to
his wife's amazement, he actually grinned. "She always
had a gift for interpretation . . . and was she not splendid?"

"Splendid?" his wife echoed in shocked tones. "Can one
think that you approved it—and she telling you she was
living in seclusion on the Continent!"

"Come, Dorcas," Sir Bertram's eyes were dancing, "she
might not have been on the Continent, but certainly she
was living in seclusion, for I vow there's nothing more
secluded than the provincial towns in which she must have
played."

"And all of poor Lord Vane's letters begging us to divulge her whereabouts if we knew them."

Sir Bertram regarded her gravely. "He blamed himself
for her flight, if you'll remember."

"Naturally, because he is a gentleman," Dorcas replied
tartly.

"I'll not have aspersions cast upon my sister," Sir Bertram said more coldly than he was wont to address her.
"I could only wish my aunt had trusted me."

A number of sentences spun themselves out in Lady
Heberdeen's head but dissolved like bubbles before they
found her tongue. To criticize yet another member of his
family would have angered him still further and he could
be edgy at times. She contented herself with saying wonderingly, "It's amazing that you've not mentioned your aunt
to me before. Were you ashamed of her?"

"No, but I feared you might be, considering your family's strong Methodist leaning." There was a hardness to
his tone. He was close to being seriously annoyed with
Dorcas and, as had happened on other occasions, though
his annoyance and his angers were brief, they left a vague
dissatisfaction with her that did not vanish easily and gave

rise to resentments he would have preferred not to entertain.

She said, "It is not only Methodists who disapprove of the acting profession. However, I hope I am not so hidebound. Will you go back to see her then?"

The look she received was so surprised and so disapproving that she realized she had erred again.

"How could I not? But if it wars with your principles, my love, you need not accompany me."

Dorcas heard a note in his voice that frightened her. "Of course I shall accompany you," she said hastily. "Though I cannot approve Anthea's actions in not informing you concerning herself and you so worried over her, I do want to see her."

Bertie still regarded her dubiously, but he produced a smile. "I thank you, my love."

With another and even more valiant effort, Lady Heberdeen managed to say, "I do agree with you that she is amazingly good as Lydia Languish."

This time his smile was genuine and grateful. "You are kind to say so, my dear."

The greenroom of the Theater Royal was located to the right of the stage and immediately after a performance that everyone praised, a number of patrons—mainly gentlemen, Lady Heberdeen noticed with some disapproval—made their way into its grass-colored interior. She, following in their wake, could not contemplate her coming proximity to a group of people she had been brought up to consider rogues and vagabonds with any enthusiasm. In spite of her brave words to her husband, she was nearly overcome with shock that he was so closely related to one or rather two of that motley crew, and here, with a little titter that she quickly turned into a cough, one could use the term "motley" and have it entirely applicable.

Oddly enough she found herslef largely unsurprised at the trick Anthea had played upon them all. She had never liked her, sly puss. She would never, never forgive her for

having come between herself and Bertie. Not for a moment
did she believe his denials. Indeed, his very pride in what
he termed Anthea's "accomplished performance," proved
that. In his estimation his sister could do no wrong—not
even when sinking to the level of a hired actress—not even
when cruelly barring the door against his betrothed when
he lay wounded and, no doubt, calling for his Dorcas.

They had crossed the threshold. Sucking in a sustaining
breath, Lady Heberdeen braced herself for the coming encounter. She cast a swift furtive glance around the chamber,
barely repressing a shudder as she saw the rubicund person
who had enacted the role of Sir Lucius O' Trigger. She did
not see her sister-in-law—so dreadful to be related by marriage to a thespian! Fortunately she was not using her own
name and if Bertie did not address her as "sister," no one
among the *ton* would be the wiser.

"Bertie!"

"Clive!"

Heads turned as these two greetings fell fast upon each
other and several interested glances rested upon the tall
handsome man in the impeccable evening attire who was
swiftly making his way toward the young man leaning upon
the crutch.

"My dear," Bertie glanced down at his wife and said
excitedly, "it's Clive Alacorn, who was in my regiment at
Waterloo. We were the greatest of friends. I've been wondering where he was."

A moment later Lady Heberdeen was having her hand
kissed by Clive Alacorn, who was also the Marquis of
Fearing. Looking into his hazel-green eyes and reading ad-
miration in them, she was sadly distressed that a man of
his obvious gentility and charm must soon know of their
regrettable connection.

Having acknowledged the introduction to Sir Bertram's
wife, the Marquis turned back to his comrade. "I would I'd
known you were here. As it is, I shall be leaving soon. My
dear Bertie, I heard you were ill and longed to visit you,

but as you know, my estate's in Northumberland and at the time poor Elsa was ill and I could not leave her."

"Elsa. I pray she is better."

The Marquis shook his head. "No, I am a widower."

"Ah," Bertie made a small sound of distress. "I am indeed sorry to hear that. She was a beautiful girl and so pleasant. How does your son fare?"

The Marquis's eyes lighted. "Very well. He is at home. He grows apace. I shall see him in another month and I expect I'll not recognize him."

"Do you visit him so seldom?" Lady Heberdeen asked.

"On the contrary, I am there quite often. But I do not exaggerate as to his height. He came to my hip one month and the next his head was nearer my waist. And at six, he's already an excellent rider and begs I bring him a horse rather than a pony, but enough. I do not mean to sound like the doting parent I am. What might you be doing here? Do you come as an admirer or a friend of an actor?"

Lady Heberdeen tensed, wishing at that moment that she were at the bottom of a fen, for there was but one answer Bertie would make and then the Marquis would know and the friendly light die from his eyes. If there were only a way to explain that until this evening they had been in total ignorance as to Anthea's dreadful actions. If only, but certainly Bertie could not explain. He would merely state it as a fact and that was what he was doing!

"My sister is in the company," he was saying as casually as if it were nothing out of the way for a baronet of ancient lineage to make such an admission, and furthermore he had the ill-grace to compound it with the added and gratuitous information, "so also is my aunt."

"You see——" Lady Heberdeen began and clamped her teeth over her tongue. What could he see? How might he understand? Surprise was already written large upon his contenance and both of them forever dimished in his eyes.

"Your sister," the Marquis repeated, "but was she not in the schoolroom?"

"She was and—" He broke off, and looking past the Marquis, he called loudly, "Anthea!"

Thea, hearing that well-remembered voice, had a moment of blank surprise as she looked about the room. Then, seeing Bertie near the door, she forgot all resolutions, all, indeed, save that he was there and that she had not seen him for two years. "Bertie," she cried brokenly and though the greenroom was even more crowded than it had been before, she was across it in an instant and caught in his embrace. "Oh, Bertie, Bertie," she half wept against his shoulder and it was not until a moment later that she was aware of Dorcas's hostile stare and from that same direction, the Marquis of Fearing's incredulous gaze.

Blinking tears from her eyes, Thea drew back, becoming aware now of those forgotten resolutions. However, it was too late for regrets—the encounter she had been dreading was upon her and with it, the need for explanations which she was singularly reluctant to provide. These, at least, could not be proffered yet, but she had to say something. In that moment Dorcas spoke.

"My dear Anthea, you were truly fine. Such a surprise, my dear, and we thought you liv—" She broke off with a little gasp.

Thea, seeing the slight movement of Bertie's crutch, guessed that Dorcas had felt its warning prod. Inadvertently she glanced at the Marquis, encountering his probing stare, grew pink.

He, in turn, looked at her brother and drawled, "Yes, Bertie my friend, your sister has indeed left the schoolroom."

"Bertie," Dolly Playfaire came up to him, smiling gaily, but Thea who knew her every look saw that her green eyes were wary. She tried to exchange glances with her aunt but failed to catch Dolly's eye—her gaze being fixed on her brother's face. "What might you be doing in Bath? Come to take the waters?"

Ignoring her question, he bent a quizzical look upon her.

"Never let it be said that females can't keep secrets."

She nodded. "I thought it for the best and still think it best that some secrets be maintained."

"Might I come to see you on the morrow?" he asked.

"I should have suggested it, if you had not," she replied.

"You must be dear Bertie's aunt." Lady Heberdeen came to stand near her husband. "I am Dorcas Heberdeen," she added with the barest trace of condescension.

"I am delighted to meet you, but you need hardly have told me that. You've much the look of your mother. When I first saw you, it gave me quite a shock. It was almost as if I were seeing Marguerite . . . young again."

"You knew my mother!" Lady Heberdeen exclaimed.

Dolly's eyes suddenly gleamed with amusement. "Very well. We were presented to the King on the same day."

"Oh," Lady Heberdeen blinked, and for want of anything else to say, smiled nervously.

The Marquis of Fearing studied Thea's face. "Your brother and I were in the same regiment at Waterloo. I remember his mentioning his sister with great affection."

She looked down. "You'll no doubt wonder . . ."

"Without doubt, I do wonder, I . . ." He broke off as Lady Heberdeen came over to them, saying sweetly, "But do you know my sister-in-law, Lord Alacorn?"

"We have an acquaintance," he acknowledged.

"Oh, lovely. We are not long in Bath, but we are staying in a charming house. I hope that all of you will be our guests for dinner."

"It would be my pleasure," he bowed.

"Anthea, my dear, you must come," Lady Heberdeen urged. "Bertie will want to have a talk with you. He, we, both have been so concerned. Say you will come, do. You must not vanish again!"

Thea said gently, "Of course I will accept your invitation, provided it is possible."

"Why would it not be possible?" There was a slight edge to Lady Heberdeen's voice.

"It must be a day on which I am not performing."

"Oh, of—of course," Lady Heberdeen said hurriedly. "I do not know how I came to forget that. But, of course, we shall arrange all according to your convenience, my dear." She darted back to her husband.

"And I," murmured the Marquis, "should also wish to arrange all according to your convenience, my dear Miss Playfaire."

She gave him a sharp look. "What may you mean by that?"

"Something quite different than I meant before," he responded, his eyes suddenly narrowed and intent. "I might add that I am very glad your brother chose to attend your performance tonight."

"I still do not understand you." She raised perplexed eyes to his.

"I do not mean that you should at this particular moment . . . but there will be other moments, Miss Playfaire. And now I shall wish you a good evening." He bowed over her hand and after bidding her brother and his wife a cordial farewell, he bowed over Dolly's hand and left the room.

5

THE HOUSE THAT Sir Bertram had hired for their visit to
Bath was located near Camden Crescent and commanded
an admirable view of the city. In addition to its agreeable
situation, it had recently been repainted and repapered and
its furnishings were charming. The appeal of the house was
such, in fact, that it had been Lady Heberdeen's private
lament that they had no acquaintances in Bath whom she
could invite to a dwelling at once so attractive and so fashionable. Though with the dinner she was giving for her
newfound relations, this state of affairs had changed, she
could not help feeling that it had been done with the dubious
aid of one of those ill-conditioned fairies made famous in
the tales of Charles Perrault.

Still, pride and the alleviating presence of the charming
Marquis of Fearing dictated that she should do her utmost

to make the evening a memorable one. Her guests were requested to come at the increasingly fashionable hour of seven. Lady Heberdeen, inspecting a table covered with a fine linen cloth, had decried the absence of the silver they had left at home. Still, the table looked very festive with the flowers she herself had arranged in a crystal bowl and the candles were in massive silver holders. Actually, though she would never have admitted such a thing to her husband, she was having second thoughts about silver she had left behind and these assured her that the table was well enough for the likes of their guests.

Furthermore she was very pleased that Sir Bertram was gone to escort his sister and his aunt thither. It was difficult to maintain an air of delighted expectancy when she could not approve what she, in her own mind, did not hesitate to term a "Descent into the Depths of Depravity." Who, among right-thinking people, she asked herself bitterly, would not agree with her?

However, since for the sake of her husband and the charming Marquis of Fearing—he *was* charming, that could not be denied, whatever the relationship he maintained with her perfidious sister-in-law—it behooved her to appear at her best. She had donned her newest gown, an ensemble that both her maid and her mirror assured her was entirely becoming. A round gown, it consisted of a rose silk slip over which fell pale violet net. It was cut low and its bodice was trimmed with pink and lavender rosettes. The puffed sleeves were adorned with knots of rose and lavender ribbons. Tiny lavender kid shoes showed off her graceful feet and, occasionally, a little surreptitious hitch to her skirt would give gentlemen the barest glimpse of her well-turned ankles. As she waited to greet her guests in the small drawing room which Bertie insisted on dubbing a "parlor," a most unwelcoming expression played over her features and if her husband had seen her, he would have been both surprised and shocked. In the two years of their marriage only the servants had been treated to a vision of Lady

Heberdeen in "fit o' the sullens," as her maid Sally described it.

"If only we'd not come to Bath," she whispered. Her regrets were doubly intense since she herself was responsible for their presence in the city. Bertie had been looking weary of late and his manner was often listless. Occasionally he had even been cross with her, answering her shortly—though, of course, he had apologized profusely afterward. She attributed his actions to his wound which, she guessed, must pain him severely from time to time, though it was definitely not in his nature to complain. Thinking of his severed leg, she sighed. Poor Bertie, who had once danced every dance with her at Almack's. He had been supremely graceful and to see him limping and—but she would not think of that. She loved him even more now that he was so dependent on her. Yet that did not mean she must love his horrid sister and it greatly pained her that she was not, under any circumstance, to reveal Anthea's whereabouts to Lord Vane. She had been horrified at this stipulation.

"But it is our duty," she had told Bertie.

"It is not our duty and now you know the reason she fled, I tell you it's our duty to remain silent."

Lady Heberdeen, who had been amazed at Titus Croydon's determined pursuit of her sister-in-law, longed to assure him that no one but a loving brother would have failed to perceive that the girl was not the sort to inspire a deathless passion. She should have been happy to have won such a man as Lord Vane, no matter what the reasons behind his offer. However, she had contented herself with saying, "Must we be silent indefinitely?"

"It is not up to us to reveal my sister's secrets."

"But should not Lord Vane and she meet and . . ."

"In my opinion it would be better if they did," Sir Bertram had interrupted, "but it must be because *she* desires it." His eyes grew somber. "She has suffered greatly, my aunt tells me."

Dorcas had longed to inform him that she could not see that Anthea was wearing the willow for Titus Croydon— not with the glances she had seen her exchange with the Marquis of Fearing. However, she had not dared argue with Bertie, not when he was in this uncompromising mood. Her resentment toward his sister increased. Obviously Anthea had brought him around to her way of thinking just as she had in the old days, when her untoward interference in their affairs had nearly separated her from Bertie forever!

"Oh, God," she cried. "Why could she not have been in seclusion as she said she was? Liar! And if she suffered so greatly, why did she not take an overdose of laudanum and put a period to her existence—'twould have been a far better solution for all concerned!" Directly upon uttering this sentiment, she gasped and brought her hand to her mouth. It was dangerous to ill-wish anyone. Her old nurse had warned her that curses come home to roost. A second later she found she could comfort herself with the fact that she had neither cursed nor ill-wished Anthea since it was too late for such hopes to be effective—and her sister-in-law whole, healthy, and an *actress*!

"Oh," she moaned, "it is not to be borne. And must I receive her in London? I shan't . . . not even if Bertie flogs me." She sighed, as she realized that she had no choice in the matter. If she were to retain her husband's respect and love, she must do exactly as he wished when it came to Anthea!

A discreet knock on the door caused her to tense and say sharply, "Well?"

Baines, her butler, appeared on the threshold. "The Marquis of Fearing, my lady," he announced.

"Ah, show him in, Baines." Her eyes gleamed. She had not expected that he would arrive before the other guests. Rising, she looked expectantly toward the door and was rewarded with his handsome presence. He was, she decided, looking even better than the other night, appearing to advantage in an evening suit of superfine black cloth. "My lord," she curtsied.

He crossed the chamber in two strides and bowed over her hand. "Your servant, Lady Heberdeen," he murmured. "Am I the first to arrive? How unfashionable of me."

"But how delightful for me," she smiled. "Please, will you not sit down." Indicating a chair, she sank gracefully upon her sofa. "My husband has gone to fetch his sister and his aunt. He should be here directly."

"Ah, is that why my services were refused?" He glanced out of the window. "You have a very pleasant location here."

"Yes, we feel ourselves most fortunate. It was by way of being an inheritance."

"A deceased relative . . ."

"No, I mean, a dear friend, Lord St. Aubyn, had hired it for the season, but he was called home and asked if we should want it. I'd been hoping that Bertie might take the waters—so I begged that he accept the offer. Otherwise I am sure we should have had considerable difficulty in obtaining the proper accommodations."

"Indeed you might," the Marquis agreed. "Bath fills very rapidly at this time of year."

"It is a pleasant city. Bertie has been enjoying the waters. I hope they may be good for him."

"Has he been ill, then?" he asked with a trace of anxiety.

"No, not ill . . . his wound," Dorcas replied, her eyes as well as her voice full of compassion.

He looked grim. "Yes, a great pity."

"But at least he lived. So many did not." She looked down. "So many families were bereaved."

"True."

"Did you know Bertie's brother Anthony?"

He shook his head. "No. He was killed at Vitoria, was he not?"

Lady Heberdeen nodded and was suddenly visited by a

flash of sheer inspiration. "And Odo, too. No, I think I am wrong. It seems to me that Anthea told me he died a natural death."

"Odo?" he inquired.

"Odo Croydon, the late Lord Vane, Anthea's brother-in-law, oh dear!" She looked up into his puzzled eyes. "I should never have said that. I have been sworn to the *deepest* secrecy and . . . and to inadvertently betray poor Anthea . . ."

"Betray her? What can you mean, Lady Heberdeen?"

Dorcas looked down, nervously pleating her skirt. "You must ask me no more. It is a *sacred* promise."

The Marquis frowned. "Odo Croydon. I am acquainted with Titus Croydon, Lord Vane, and was not Odo a member of the Four-in-Hand Club?"

"I—I do not know anything about him," she said in a small unhappy voice. "I know very little about the family. I wish to know very little about them. Oh, dear." Dorcas fixed her eyes on her guest. "I know I have no right to ask this, my lord, but I pray you'll say nothing of what I—I have told you to Bertie or Anthea. It would be disastrous for me. Bertie would be so angry and rightly. I—think he might never forgive me."

"But you've said nothing save that . . .," he paused. "Anthea's brother-in-law? Was she wed to Titus Croydon, then?"

"Oh, dear." She wrung her hands and looked down.

"And is yet wed to him?" the Marquis pursued.

"Yes, but only in *name*. Lord Vane must have been very cruel, else I am sure she would not have fled. Those who hint that the fault was hers are quite, quite in error. There was never another man involved—the fault was Lord Vane's. Knowing Anthea, I can believe nothing else." She gazed at his concerned face through lashes which, at that moment, were bedewed with the tears she could produce to very telling effect when necessary.

"I see," he mused.

"You should not see. You should not know anything—anything," Dorcas sobbed.

"But since I do, Lady Heberdeen, perhaps you will tell me . . . did this marriage last long?"

"Not above three days, but I pray you'll not divulge this knowledge to anyone, especially not to Lord Vane, for he is not to know her whereabouts. I cannot think what might happen to her if he were to find out."

"Yet if he were to go to the theater . . ."

"I think he is not often in town—but please, we must not talk of this. They will be arriving soon and before they come, you must promise you'll not breathe a word of what I have told you. I did not mean that you should know it. Oh, my unguarded tongue. Please . . . please, say nothing." She fixed beseeching eyes upon his face.

"Come," the Marquis said soothingly, "you must know that I would never betray you by word or action, my dear Lady Heberdeen."

"Oh, I do thank you, my lord, and pray do not think ill of my inadvertent betrayal. I would not for the world do *anything* to harm poor Anthea. You must believe that I, above all people, have always had her best interests at heart. She is a dear good girl, if a little wild sometimes, as witness her going on the stage—but really there's not a particle of harm in her."

Dorcas was saved from further protestations by the sound of her husband's voice in the hall and by Anthea's laughter. Looking at the Marquis of Fearing, she saw that he was frowning. As the door opened upon her other guests, she was pleasantly sure that, in addition to the very good dinner she would soon be serving him, she had given the Marquis an ample supply of food for thought.

Lady Cornelia, emerging from her chamber on a morning in late May, was amazed and displeased to find her son, dressed for traveling and preceded by a footman who was hurrying down the stairs with two portmanteaus. Titus had only recently returned from an extended stay on the Continent—four months, in fact, of journeying through France, Switzerland, and Italy. He had come home looking weary, dissatisfied, and dispirited. He had promised that he would remain in residence at Vane for an indefinite period. Obviously, she thought bitterly, their interpretation of "indefinite" differed widely since she had taken it to mean months rather than a mere three weeks. Forestalling him at the head of the stairs, she said as much in tones that were both querulous and disapproving.

He heard her patiently but at the end of her diatribe, he said, merely, "I am going no further than London."

"But there is so much to be done here, my dear. The estate agent and . . ."

"And you are quite capable of dealing with Mr. Soames, Mother."

"Do you not think it high time that you settled down and took the reins of the estate in your two hands? I shall not last forever, you know."

A corner of his mouth twitched. "I imagine you will last the length of my stay in London."

"And how long might that be?"

"I am not sure."

"That is not a very satisfactory answer."

"I can provide no other."

"When you came home, you told me . . ."

"I know," he interrupted, "but since then I have changed my mind."

"It must have been since yesterday, then, for you said nothing of any such journey at supper last night."

His eyes hardened. "I am sorry that I failed to confide my plans, Mother," he said with unmistakable sarcasm, "but suffice to say that there are matters in London which require my immediate attention. Now if you will excuse me, I think that by now my curricle has been brought round and I am sure that the horses will be straining at their bits. If I am detained longer than I anticipate, I shall send word."

Giving her a hasty peck on the cheek, he added, "Good-bye, Mother."

He was down the stairs so quickly that Lady Cornelia found she was holding her breath as he reached the bottom. The perilous speed of his descent brought back a memory. As a child, Titus had moved with that particular swiftness only when he was excited. It also occurred to her that if she had not come out of her chamber at that particular moment, he would have gone without a word, which was certainly unlike him. Something must have happened and she quite burned to know what it was. She hurried down the stairs but as she emerged from the front door, the pebbles on the driveway were already flying into the air under the stimulus of his curricle wheels as he expertly tooled that vehicle toward the beech-lined avenue that led to the park. At the momentum at which he was moving, he would be on the highway in a very short time. Lady Cornelia ground her teeth. Not for the first time she wished that Titus had possessed the tractable disposition of Odo—dear Odo, who had obeyed her every wish without protest and who never would have left his mother wondering futilely what he had up his admirably tailored sleeve.

Drury Lane, bright with lights and well-filled for the performance of *As You Like It*—which, so report had it, would present an actress of an age comparable with that of Rosalind, rather than someone of the forty-odd-year-old females who had essayed it. That was enough to raise anticipation and, at the same time, doubt, since the idea of a young unknown woman in that difficult part roused considerable skepticism among seasoned theater patrons. Bets had been laid at White's as to the success of Miss Thea Playfaire and the odds were known to be against her. Some dandies, hearing that the newcomer was beautiful, were placing other more informal bets as to which among their number would ultimately become her Protector. Rumors concerning a friendship with the Marquis of Fearing had already reached the ears of the *ton* and that was enough to discourage some of the younger men who laid siege to every pretty actress who stepped upon the boards. The Marquis had enjoyed several liaisons with these beauties and was known to possess not only a formidable charm but a well-lined purse, two assets which generally gained him anything or anyone he wanted.

Titus Croydon was seated in the box he had obtained only by the exchange of a considerable sum of money over the ticket price. It was a transaction which annoyed him. He was not there to view the play but to meet the writer of a certain blotted missive which had come by messenger early that morning. He scanned the boxes, searching for that writer but not seeing her. In his mind's eye he could still envision the letter which, at her urgent and, to his mind, melodramatic request, he had destroyed immediately upon perusing. Words such as loyalty, disloyalty, pain of death, and duty had cluttered every barely decipherable sentence and were underlined two or three times. It had been penned by little Lady Heberdeen, a chit for whom he had scant liking. It specified that he meet her during the First Interval of *As You Like It*, being sure, in case her husband was present, to act as if he were considerably surprised to see them. However, she hoped that Sir Bertram would remain in his box as was his wont, while she would be waiting at the head of the first staircase. At that time she would have information about his vanished wife. It had contained the further intelligence that he must not, under any circumstance, ever let Sir Bertram learn of her confidence.

A deep frown creased his brow. The clandestine nature of this projected meeting both angered and confused him. If Lady Heberdeen had received information concerning his lost wife, why need it be kept secret from her brother? And how had she managed to discover anything about Anthea while that same brother remained ignorant? And what did that obscure reference to duty and loyalty signify? But above all what did she know about Anthea? What had happened to her? This question had plagued him for two years; now it seemed as if it might have an answer! Yet what manner of answer? At present, seated on a deucedly uncomfortable chair in his box, he was caught among expectancy, fear, and anger. He had searched for her so long and so fruitlessly!

Sir Bertram had told him of places where they had gone as children—he had gone there, too. He had followed such leads as interviewing retired servants, nurses, nursery maids, and, he winced in retrospect, Mrs. Peterson, her old governess, a stern female who had fixed a steely eye upon him and acidly inquired as to what he had done to cause that "sweet creature" to flee? He had endeavored to give her a strong setdown but before her accusing glare, his words had faltered to silence.

Subsequently he had learned from Sir Bertram that she was living "in seclusion upon the Continent." He had gone to cities where there were large English colonies. Paris, Geneva, Florence, Rome had been scoured, not once but twice. He had only recently returned from such an expidition, driven by a sense of guilt, a sense of having been both cruel and cowardly and, above all, of having betrayed one for whom he had already formed a great affection.

Of course Rosalie's ill-timed confidence had not helped matters. His old fury at her interference arose and diminished, for in fact, he could not blame her. He could only blame himself. Anthea had surprised him that night. She had been unexpectedly passionate, but he had been haunted by Guilia and the shy caresses his bride had given him had only aroused memories of Guilia's fingers stroking his body. Her loving little words had echoed in his ears—those Italian endearments, her giving nature, at the time so entirely different from anything he had ever experienced.

He had fallen in love with Guilia at first sight. Her sweetness, her beauty had proved enough to make him renounce his home, his name, his world. As Tito—she had called him Tito—Manders, he had been received into her family, her warm, loving family, which had no trouble expressing their affections, who had welcomed him and with whom he could be himself. He had never dreamed that such warmth could exist. It had seemed, indeed, that the di Rossis inhabited another sphere than that of the cold, ordered world of his childhood. Though his mother had loved his brother and himself, she had never lavished the caresses or the praise upon either of her sons that Signora di Rossi had freely divided among her three boys and two daughters. Signor di Rossi had been equally affectionate with his children and Titus, remembering his own self-contained and distant father, had been confounded!

The di Rossis, expelled from their native Rome because of political activities, were not rich. Even though Carlo di Rossi was a member of the minor nobility, he had been forced to support himself as a fencing master, which was how Titus had met him. Yet he had been amazingly generous, willing to share his small substance with Titus and, in accepting him as a fencing instructor, he had divided his income still further. It had not been easy work, especially since Titus Croydon, though only recently arrived in London, had some acquaintance among the *ton*, men who knew his background and who, in common with his mother, could not understand his marriage or his flight from respectability. He had endured cuts and snubs, but nothing had mattered as long as Guilia awaited him in the small chamber at the top of the ramshackle old house, half fencing academy and half lodgings for the family, in Chelsea Village.

He had been gloriously, incredibly happy in those constricted quarters. Then Guilia had whispered to him the wonderful news that she was expecting a child, a child, which, she had insisted must be his son. He had tenderly protested, telling her that he wanted a daughter who would be as beautiful as her mother—though, he had added, he doubted that were possible.

There had followed nine happy months of preparation—of sewing minute garments, of readying the cradle that would be set close to Guilia's side of the bed, and then, at the last, the pain, the terror, and her lying pale, agonized, exhausted from bearing the heavy but pallid child. Upon uttering one feeble cry his son had expired, minutes before his mother, raising dimming eyes to her husband's face, had murmured in the failing whisper he could still remember, "Ees a fine *bambino, si*? A leetle Tito."

"A fine son, my darling," he had told her, "*bellissimo, mia cara*."

"Ah, *sono felice* . . . so happy, *mio caro* . . ." Her last look had been one of mingled love and regret. Then with a long, weary sigh, she had died.

Shortly thereafter the tiny chamber had been filled with as many of her family as could crowd into its narrow confines. Her father had fallen to his knees beside the bed, her mother had collapsed at his side, their unrestrained grief loud in his ears. He had recoiled from the lot of them, finding their sobs and moans distasteful—even theatrical. His own grief was deeper. He could not express it, could not revel in it, as they seemed to be doing. For the first time he realized that among these people he was an alien. The sense of loss he experienced was tripled. In addition to his wife and his child, he had lost his adopted family as well. He could not live with them.

Immediately after Guilia's funeral he had gone away, traveling throughout England, living frugally and supporting himself by working as a horse trainer, a riding master, and as a tutor. Finally he had returned to London and, coming to see Signor di Rossi, he had learned that his brother Odo had died and that his mother was searching for him.

He had gone back to Vane and made peace with Lady Cornelia, but he should have known that five years was not long enough to expunge the memory of his shared happiness

with Guilia. Poor Anthea, whom he had found to be such
a good companion, one who could make him laugh, had
been the sufferer.

It had been such a difficult day, his wedding day. He
had been beset with memories of kneeling in the small
Roman church next to Guilia in the long lace veil which
had once belonged to her great-grandmother. The candles
had illuminated her beautiful, happy face. He had thought
she resembled the picture of the Madonna on the wall to
his right. There had been no pictures of Madonnas in the
austere interior of St. Martin-in-the-Fields and when the
minister has asked for his responses, he had felt as if he
were betraying his real wife. Then, in riding to Vane, he
had managed to brush these cobwebs out of his head. While
riding, he had always obtained a clearer perspective on
matters which troubled him.

He had gone to Anthea, determined to make the most
of his marriage. It had not been as difficult as he had imagined until those shy little caresses, which had recalled Guilia. He knew he must have hurt her deeply when he had
fled from her bed, but he could not help it. He had gone
to London early the following morning, to Guilia's grave
and to see her family. They had been the same—but their
noisy reception had chilled him. He had been glad he was
no longer a part of their circle and he had had the terrible
fear that if Guilia had lived, her outgoing manner might
also have palled on him. He had dismissed this heresy from
his mind quickly, but he had found himself anxious to return
to Anthea—and then, he had found her gone. It had been
a terrible shock—especially since he had no idea what had
happened to her.

There had been times when he had feared that all women
who loved him were accursed—which, of course, was pure
Byronic nonsense. His lip curled. He had always laughed
at Lord Byron's moody extravagances. He had little respect
for a man he believed to be a poseur and, having had a
passing acquaintance with Lady Caroline Lamb, he believed

him to be cruel and heartless as well. Yet he could scarcely level such an accusation at the poet without including himself in that indictment.

Sighing, he cast another glance around the auditorium and tensed as he saw Sir Bertram and Lady Heberdeen taking their seats in a box situated directly across from his own. He looked fixedly in their direction but failed to catch Sir Bertram's eye. He, in turn, was looking expectantly at the curtain. He was sure, however, that Lady Heberdeen had seen him, for her unquiet eyes had darted about the boxes. She had not looked directly at him. That, he thought with a grim little smile, was not surprising given the panics and precautions of her letter. His impatience mounted. He longed to disobey her instructions and make his way to her side immediately, but that, of course, would have been contrary to all codes of proper behavior. He had to wait.

The curtain was rising and he grimaced. He had never been partial to *As You Like It*. As he had once told his tutor, it need not be incumbent upon a person to love every word penned by Shakespeare. To his mind, the fact that Orlando had not been able to recognize the "youth" Ganymede as the woman he loved, merely because she had donned men's clothing, was ridiculous. That went for Portia, Imogen, Viola, and the lot. He prepared himself for boredom, double boredom since the woman who would enact the Rosalind— Thea Playfaire—was an unknown quantity. A glance at the program had informed him that it was her London debut after tremendous successes throughout England and Scotland. He was unimpressed by this intelligence. He had seen numerous provincial hopefuls come in the words of Wordsworth, "trailing clouds of glory," only to be hooted from the stage. He moved restlessly and then, as the curtain rose, he fixed his resentful gaze on stupid Orlando, who was entering with an Adam so feeble that it seemed the man would collapse ere he had uttered his first word. With a sigh he leaned back in his chair—wishing that it were more comfortable, for then he could sleep.

6

THE AUDITORIUM RANG with cheers. She, who had been uncertain, had been swallowing countless air bubbles, who had, in fact, suffered all the disquieting symptoms of a virulent attack of stage fright, bowed, smiled, and bowed again taking curtain call after curtain call. By the time the audience was prepared to release her, she felt both limp and exhilarated—too limp to protest when, as she came off the stage, the Marquis of Fearing, privileged by class and by the exchange of coins to wait in the wings, gathered her into his arms and kissed her on the lips—murmuring a long moment later. "Madame Siddons could have done no better, my love."

Thea raised dazzled, unseeing eyes to his face, thinking she ought to protest a familiarity she had always forbidden, but found she had neither the energy nor the inclination to push him away. His sustaining arm felt definitely comfortable to one who had eschewed that particular comfort for such a long time. His words had fallen sweetly on her ears. And, if his kiss had not roused the excitement she had experienced with the man she had once called "husband," she warmed to him to the point where she could cling to him a second before she was surrounded by her admiring colleagues, the manager of the theater, by her aunt, and her dresser. She was swept in triumph to her dressing room, while the Marquis smilingly promised to await her in the greenroom.

"My dearest," Dolly, hovering over Thea as she creamed off her makeup, said, "I was so proud of you! You surpassed yourself which, though you may not deem it so, is the highest praise I could proffer."

Thea smiled vaguely at her. She was still transported by the applause, by the acclaim she had received from her peers, and by the Marquis's embrace which had provided a feeling of safety. From the bulwark of his body she was suddenly aware that she need not fear anything or anyone. With a little shock she realized she had not felt really safe since she had fled from Vane all those years ago—but it had not been that long. It had been only two years and a little over, but it had been a very hectic and strange period for one born to wealth and position. She had need to become adjusted to the casual manners and mores of her fellow thespians, to living in indifferent lodgings, to ignoring the jeers and catcalls of rude audiences, to repulsing the familiarities of country yokels and of leering noblemen who believed any actress must provide rare sport. It had been very difficult, but it had also helped erase the agonizing memory of her wedding night and its demeaning aftermath. Still the Marquis's embrace had an element of danger in it, too. She was not free to wed him—even if he would have asked her, which she doubted. And she would not—could not—be his mistress!

"Thea . . . Thea . . ." Dolly said, "what are you about,

child? You cannot sit there dreaming. They'll be waiting for you, clamoring for you. Come, you must hurry."

"I'm sorry, Aunt Dolly," she smiled. "I was not thinking..."

"On the contrary, my dear, I should say that you were thinking far too much. Fearing's a most attractive man but you should not have allowed such liberties unless..."

"I know," Thea interrupted quickly. "I shall not do so again. It was only that he was waiting there. I was taken by surprise."

Dolly nodded understandingly. "One is never quite conscious after coming off stage at the end of a performance... especially after such a triumph."

"True," Thea dutifully agreed, but she had been conscious of Fearing and that sense of being protected still prevailed. If anyone could help obliterate the persistent image of Titus Croydon, it would be the Marquis. She winced, thinking of that presence which, appearing in dreams, brought tears. These, upon awakening, remained on her cheeks to be indignantly, even furiously, wiped away. She flushed. Again her thoughts were tending in the wrong direction. She ought to be concentrating solely on her recent acclaim, but that did not seem nearly as important as that which had happened directly following her final bow.

There was another factor, too. She had not expected to find the Marquis there. Since they had parted in Bath, she had not seen him. Usually he had followed her back to London, but on this occasion he had gone to his northern estates and though she had been preparing for her debut, she had missed him. In a relatively short time he had, she realized ruefully, become a part of her life— a good friend if nothing more...

"Thea, love," Dolly prompted impatiently. "Do hurry."

"Yes, Aunt." She was glad of this second interruption. She did not want to think, to speculate, to wonder. This was not the time for it. She arose from the table to let her dresser clothe her in a simple white muslin gown, a great contrast to the fancy ensembles preferred by the Celia and the Audrey—but as Dolly observed, an excellent frame for her beauty.

"You are in looks tonight, my dear," Dolly remarked as they started up the stairs from the basement dressing rooms. "It seems to me that you are even lovlier than you were on stage."

"Oh, please," Thea protested, "you do refine too much upon my appearance, Aunt Dolly."

"I cannot believe that possible. I have feared that you were a little too thin and wraithlike, but it does become you. I've never seen your eyes so large. I can understand why the Marquis could not resist your fatal fascinations."

Thea blushed. "You are teasing me," she chided. Moving a little ahead of her relative, she reached the door of the greenroom, stepping inside to a burst of spontaneous applause. Smiling and murmuring her thanks, she looked about her and found her brother standing near the Marquis. Meeting the latter's ardent gaze, she flushed and, turning away, stiffened. She came to a dead stop when she found herself staring into the eyes of Titus Croydon.

Dolly, just behind her, glimpsed her white set features. "My dear," she cried, "what is the matter? Shall I fetch the hartshorn?"

Thea did not answer. All at once the room seemed emptied, the babble silenced and only two people present, herself and the man she had not seen for two years.

He came forward to seize her suddenly nerveless hand, to lift it to his lips, and to say, "That was a most remarkable performance, Miss Playfaire. It has given me an entirely new vision of Rosalind. I had never enjoyed the play before this night."

Was he mocking her? No, there was a ring of sincerity in his words—but that did not matter. Looking at this man, hearing his voice again, she had a sense of unreality, as if she were yet caught in one of her painful dreams—but she was not dreaming. He was there, looking a little older. He was older, two years older, and there were a few threads of white at his temples—surely he was too young for that, not more than thirty. Had he been ill? There were hollows beneath his eyes. Why should that concern her? It did *not* concern her, not at all! He had no right to be standing right in front of her at the very moment of her triumph. What mischance had brought him thither? Had it been a mere coincidence? Had Bertie thought it his duty to inform him of her whereabouts? No, she was sure her brother would never have been so disloyal. Dorcas? No use, no time to speculate. He was there. She must needs speak to him.

Out of the corner of her eye, she saw her aunt approaching. Beckoning to her, she said casually, "Aunt Dolly, may I present the Earl of Vane."

"Delighted, your lordship," Dolly murmured.

"Your servant, ma'am," he bowed, while he pondered on the impersonal note he had detected in Anthea's tones as well as the glance which had held neither nervousness nor rancor. She was, indeed, regarding him with an unnerving serenity.

Anger welled up in his breast as he recalled the nagging fears he had entertained concerning her possible fate. All the time he had been imagining her in want or—even dead, she had been perfecting an art which, unless he were seriously mistaken, must make her the toast of London. How had she come by it? It was incredible! No, not really. The moment in the library came back to him, when she had aped his mother's tones to such telling effect. The talent had been there—it had only wanted bringing out. And her appearance! Shy, awkward Anthea Heberdeen transformed into a poised, beautiful—extremely beautiful—woman! She had looked almost too beautiful to be Rosalind, yet she had been splendid in the role.

He had been perfectly sincere when he had described her performance as "remarkable." She had made the play come alive for him—at least, she had after he had recovered from the shocking revelation which had caused him to lose large

portions of the first act. Indeed, he actually had had more
than a little in common with the despised Orlando; he had
not recognized her. Then, as the astounding fact that Thea
Playfaire was Anthea Croydon had inserted itself into his
consciousness, his racing thoughts, his fevered speculations
had sealed him into a cocoon of silence. He had emerged
from it angry, confused, and uncertain of what course to
pursue. There had actually been one rage-filled moment
when he had considered rushing backstage to confront her
in the wings. Fortunately common sense had prevented this
cruelty and he had finally managed to fix his mind on the
play. It was no mean tribute to her ability that he had
succeeded in so doing.

He had not sought out Lady Heberdeen during the interval; he had a very good notion that he would not find
her. He had seen her only when he had entered the greenroom. She had been standing near the door, and she had
directed a quick but telling look in his direction before
shifting her attention to her husband's face.

He frowned. Sir Bertram had appeared amazed and far
from pleased to see him. His manner had been cold as, with
some reluctance, he had explained that until a chance visit
to Bath, a fortnight previously, he had had no notion of his
sister's activities. However, he had provided the explanation
Titus required. Anthea had fled to their aunt, whose theatrical connections had been a closely guarded family secret.
He had not informed him as to why he had failed to communicate this discovery to his sister's husband, though from
the chill that had prevailed throughout their conversation,
Titus guessed that Anthea must have confided the reasons
behind that precipitate departure. He had a very good notion
that from being pitied as a wronged husband, he had, at
least in Sir Bertram's estimation, become extremely culp-
able. He longed to set matters straight, but what might he
have offered by way of an apology?

Everything he had done regarding Anthea had been
wrong. Yet to try and convey to Sir Bertram his own con-

fusion at that time would have been very difficult and, at that moment, it hardly mattered. What did matter was that he had found his wife and that they must arrive at some manner of understanding. What this might be, he was not sure. He would need to recover his own equilibrium before he could address himself to that subject. He could wish that Mrs. Playfaire, who was undoubtedly the actress aunt who had sheltered her, was not present. He did not appreciate her critical stare. Obviously she must share Sir Bertram's feelings. In a low voice he said, "It is necessary that we meet again, Miss Playfaire...perhaps tomorrow?"

Negation flared in her eyes. "That would not be possible, sir," she replied sharply.

"Dolly, my love," someone called in the rich fruity tones of the professional actor.

"Henry!" Dolly smiled brightly at Titus. "If you will excuse me...an old friend."

"Of course, ma'am," he bowed again, waiting until she was out of earshot before saying, "Anthea, I pray you, if not tomorrow, at your convenience. We have much to say to each other."

Her blue eyes glittered with an icy radiance as she told him, "I cannot agree with you, sir. I cannot think of anything that I wish to say to you."

"Then, I pray you will hear me. If you but knew how..." He paused, for the Marquis of Fearing, a man with whom he had a passing acquaintance, had come to stand beside his wife. Annoyed at this second interruption, he said coldly, "Good evening, Fearing."

The Marquis's greeting proved equally chill. "Good evening, Vane."

Titus saw a look of consternation flicker briefly in Anthea's eyes before she said lightly, "You are acquainted, then, my lords?"

"We are," Titus snapped and was immediately annoyed with himself for this far from gracious rejoinder.

The Marquis, on the other hand, was urbanity itself, as

he smilingly acknowledged, "Yes, we've boxed together at Cribb's Parlor and last fall we bid against each other at Tattersall's. I was bested in that exchange. I hope you are finding the filly worth the blunt you gave for her, Vane."

"She's a fine animal," Titus returned. He was aware from looks passing between his wife and Fearing that they knew each other well. He could not approve such a friendship. Fearing's penchant for pretty actresses was common knowledge. He had been present when bets upon his success with a certain Mrs. Bartlett had been laid at Watier's and he knew that many town wags insisted that he changed his mistresses as often as Drury Lane did its playbills. His interior anger bubbled up alarmingly as the Marquis, smiling at Thea, said, "My dear, is it not time that we were on our way?"

It seemed to Titus that Anthea looked surprised but she said quickly and with an unmistakable relief, "Yes, of course." Her glance, as cool and impersonal as it had been briefly warm when resting on the Marquis's face, shifted toward him. "I pray you will excuse me, my lord." Placing her hand upon the Marquis's arm, she let him escort her in the direction of the door.

Staring after her, Titus heard a slight gasp. He looked down to find Lady Heberdeen near him. She was also watching the progress of her sister-in-law and Fearing, and it seemed to him that he could read a most unwelcome supposition in her speaking eyes.

Of course, they could not leave the theater without their way being blocked by hosts of well-wishers. Thea, acknowledging a hail of compliments, was doubly glad of the Marquis's sustaining presence. She was particularly grateful that he had removed her from the proximity of her husband but all the while she was automatically responding to her admirers, her thoughts remained on Titus Croydon.

If only he had not reemerged at this moment—in the very

hour of her success! It had turned her triumph into ashes, for it promised complication upon complication. The truth must soon be revealed and the man beside her informed of her marriage. A memory of his kiss arose in her mind. She sighed. She could expect no more kisses once he knew she had lied to him. No, she had not precisely lied, she had just not told him the truth. But either way her behavior could not be adjudged honorable. Titus's face dominated her thinking again—his handsome face, but she must not dwell on that! A quotation from *The Witch of Orange*, a play in which she had recently appeared, occurred to her. "'Twas the devil got him a handsome face, good sirs, to beguile this poor wench."

In the character of Angela, she had thus pleaded with her stern Puritan judges only to be condemned to die on the scaffold—a very telling scene. Some members of the audience had gasped in horror as they beheld the headsman, clad in scarlet, his face obscured by a black mask. Everyone had wept as she knelt to lay her head on the block. In all, it had been a most successful occasion, but why had she thought of it at this moment? Titus. Yes, his face, too, might have been sent by the devil to torment her. Her eyes hardened. Handsome is as handsome does and he had acted the devil with her. She had not known how very much she hated him until she had seen him standing before her, his eyes accusing. How dared he have looked at her in that manner, after all she had suffered at his hands?

"My dear Thea, what have I done to warrant such angry glances?" the Marquis inquired mildly.

Startled, she looked about her to find that they were out of the greenroom and in a sequestered alcove near the stage. He must have brought her there without her even being aware of it! "Oh, I—I was thinking," she stuttered.

He put his arm around her shoulders, "My poor Thea, did the sight of your husband disturb you so much?"

"My h-husband?" she gasped, staring at him incredulously. "You knew?"

"I knew," he assured her gently. "And, in consequence, I thought it up to me to play the role of St. George and save you from your dragon."

"My—dragon?" A pang shot through her and for a brief second she was back in that darkened library and a young man was rising from a chair—no, she banished him into the oblivion where he belonged.

"I—er hoped I acted in accordance with your wishes," the Marquis frowned.

"You did," she assured him emphatically. "But how did you know?" An unwelcome suspicion came to her. "Bertie?"

"Not Bertie, my dear. You must not ask me the source of my information for I've promised not to divulge it."

"Dorcas," she said positively.

"I'll not play guessing games with you, my love. Suffice to say that I am aware of your trouble and am also of the opinion that I am in the position to extricate you from it."

"Indeed? How might you do that?" Before he could respond, she had added dolefully, "I am wed, Clive."

"And may be unwed. Unless I am greatly mistaken, this marriage was of uncommonly short duration."

"You are not mistaken. I remained under his roof no more than three days—though I feel I need not tell you what you know already. I doubt, however, that you were given the proper reasons for my behavior."

"I do not need those reasons. Knowing you, I cannot imagine that they were other than ... proper."

Sudden tears pricked her eyes. "You are kind."

"Honest," he amended. Putting a finger under her chin, he tilted her face toward him. "Thea, in the time I have known you, I have grown to respect as well as love you."

"L-Love me?" she breathed.

"But surely you guessed that, my dear," he said reasonably. "How could a man remain in your sphere and not be moved by that tender passion? I have loved you for a long time, but—and here I must confess to something I'd as lief not divulge. Yet, I am sure that you are not ignorant of the fact that I wanted to give you my protection."

She blushed. "Yes, I knew that, but..."

"But you had no intention of accepting it," he finished. "I must confess I was both angered and confused by your attitude. I thought you not indifferent to me." He paused, regarding her intently. "I hope I am correct in this assumption?"

"You are correct," she murmured, the memory of his kiss large in her mind.

"Oh, my dear," passion thickened his tone and he held out his arms only to drop them hastily. "I must not embrace you again, else I could not let you go. Thea, from the first moment we met, I have been in torment. I have wanted you, but you must understand that a man in my position could not offer for an actress, no matter how virtuous she might be and no matter what his own feelings were. My family name must needs be considered and also my son, but that barrier has been removed. I pray you will not think too hardly of me—for my stand."

"Of course not, Clive." Oddly she thought of Titus and his Guilia, the woman for whose love he had renounced rank and wealth. Of course, he had been very young and obviously impetuous. The Marquis was neither and, as he had said, there was his son to be considered. She felt a twinge of annoyance. Why was Titus invading her thoughts, especially at a moment when, unless she were badly mistaken, the Marquis was about to make a most important and welcome declaration? *Especially* since her brief moment with the man she had once been so thrilled to call "husband" had proved beyond all doubt that he had lost the power to attract her? She fixed her eyes upon the Marquis's face.

"I knew you would understand," he was continuing. "We are of the same worlds, after all." His voice deepened and softened. "Thea, you cannot realize what that revelation has meant to me. I love you and though I still have no right to say it, I want your hand in marriage."

"Oh..." Even though she had felt him primed to make

such an offer, she was excited by it. "Oh, Clive," she murmured and, for some reason she could not name, she blinked back a sudden wetness from her eyes.

Seizing her hands, he said, "Would you . . . will you accept me as your husband . . . when you are free, my dearest?"

For the first time he sounded a little unsure of himself. Her heart warmed to him for that. But her tortured brain sternly reminded her that she was not free. "If . . . if I were unencumbered, I would—" She paused as he pressed her hands to his lips. "But, Clive, how could you face the scandal of a divorce?" she faltered.

"There need be no scandal and no divorce. Given your circumstances, there need be only an annulment."

"An annulment," she repeated wonderingly. "Might my marriage be annulled?"

"Yes, if it were not consummated."

She looked away quickly. Embarrassment brought a deep flush to her cheeks and disappointment clouded her tones as she answered, "But—that is not the way of it, Clive."

He was still holding her hands and he caressed them gently as he said, "I'd assumed it was not, my dear. How could it be, indeed? But you left him after three days. If he is any kind of gentleman, he will allow the motion to stand uncontested. We must put it to him once you are returned from your engagement in Birmingham. I cannot imagine that he will refuse."

"Oh," she brightened. "I am sure he will not. He did not love me."

"The more fool he," the Marquis commented harshly.

A vision of herself as she had been two years previously flickered before her mind's eye. She could easily have produced an explanation for Titus Croydon's so-called foolishness. However, all things considered, she did not, and though it was certainly the very pinnacle of impropriety, she submitted to her second kiss of the evening—assuring herself that she found it perfectly delightful!

* * *

Watching his wife as she moved through the greenroom leaning on the arm of the Marquis, Titus's anger changed to amazement at her grace. Seeing her acknowledge the compliments of her admirers, he could add graciousness to this encomium. How could a mere two years have wrought such a change? She was so beautiful! Everything about her was beautiful—her clustering golden curls, now fashionably coiffed, her deep blue eyes, her white skin, her slender shape! He had particularly approved her gown—simple but so becoming. Unknowingly he was in agreement with Dolly Playfaire as he contrasted it with the frills and furbelows donned by other actresses in the company. It was no wonder that the Marquis of Fearing had singled her out.

Thinking of his gaze as it had lingered on her face brought Titus's teeth together with an audible click. Coupled with that was the look he had glimpsed in Lady Heberdeen's eyes. Did she imagine they were lovers? *Were* they? No, it could not be possible. No matter what Anthea called herself, she was a Heberdeen—a *Croydon* he corrected himself. Furthermore there was her brother, whose pride in her was obvious. From what he knew of Sir Bertram Heberdeen, he would never contenance an illicit alliance. She and Fearing could be nothing more than friends—but again, he could not approve that friendship! He would have liked to warn her, but she would never listen to him. His old anger at Rosalie's interference was ignited once more. If she had not spoken, Anthea would never . . .

No, it was not Rosalie's fault that Anthea had left him. The fault was his alone and how might he rectify it if she would not see him? If she could be made to understand, there was a chance that the marriage might be resumed. She had loved him and he . . . he had to see her. He must obtain her direction from her brother or failing that, his wife. He looked around the room and found to his annoyance that while he had stood there lost in thought, Sir Bertram and his lady had departed. However, there was her aunt. But another searching glance revealed that she, too, had gone.

Yet it would not be difficult to obtain such information from the manager of her company.

Loud feminine laughter smote his ears and he saw that Mrs. Eddington, the young woman who had enacted the role of Audrey, was only a step away from him. Very possibly she could tell him where Anthea lived. He was about to turn toward her when a snatch of conversation gave him pause. Mr. Newbold, a well-known critic was saying, "But she will not be appearing as Rosalind again, not this season. On the morrow, one hears, she will take coach to Birmingham for some performances of *Jane Shore*. If it were not such a tedious long way, I vow I should follow her. She is a coming thing, my dear Ponsby, and if Harold Newbold says so, you may believe it."

Titus's eyes sparkled. He could not believe his good fortune at overhearing this most excellent piece of information! Given the snail-like crawl of the cumbersome mail coaches that wended their way to Birmingham, it would be a day and a night before it reached its destination. It was several years since poverty had necessitated his availing himself of such transportation but its numerous discomforts remained in his memory. Not the least of these was the narrowness of its interior. Closeted with him, she must speak to him—she would have no alternative.

Smiling, he strode forth from the overheated confines of the greenroom. He still did not know what he intended to say to Anthea once he had achieved his purpose—but first things first. He would dispatch his valet to make the necessary arrangements. He was highly pleased with himself. A proverb that Signor di Rossi had been fond of quoting came back to him, "*Al villano, la appo in mano*," which meant that in dealing with a stubborn person, one must be equally stubborn.

7

THOUGH THEA PLAYFAIRE had portrayed the unhappy Jane Shore on several occasions, she was still not sure of her lines and she had been studying the script and repeating them during much of the time it took to reach Birmingham. Consequently she was more than grateful that she had not needed to suffer the endless chattering and clamor that invariably was the portion of a mail-coach passenger. Though both she and her aunt had cherished some doubts as to the propriety of accepting the Marquis of Fearing's invitation to travel to that town in his well-sprung post chaise, while he accompanied the vehicle on horseback, the comforts promised by such a journey had served to vanquish their scruples.

Sitting in the parlor of their lodgings, close to New Street where the theater was located, Dolly smiled at Thea. "I vow 'tis the first time I've not arrived stiff as a new jackknife."

" 'I will give up mankind . . . Forget . . .' er forget?" Pages were rattled as Thea flicked through her script. "Ah, yes, 'forget the transports of increasing passion and all the pangs we feel for its decay.' There! I was not sure of that passage, but I see I am right." She turned to her aunt, "What did you say?"

"I said I'd found it a most pleasant journey. Good horses, a good meal at the inn, good company." She directed a sharp look at her niece. "Shall you continue to keep it, then?"

"Keep what?"

"The company, though I am sure I did not need to explain myself."

Thea blushed. "I do like him."

"He is likable. Many people have found him so."

Thea gave her a long look. "Are you warning me against him, still?"

"I do not know."

"You do not know? What manner of answer's that?"

"Well," Dolly studied her nails, "I should warn you were your circumstances other than they are—or he ignorant of them as he was when he pressed you to become his mistress. However, I can say that he has been constant longer than ever I can remember. Many a poor girl of my acquaintance has wept óver him. But perhaps he's sown all his wild oats and covets a better grain."

Thea's blush deepened. She picked up her playscript. "I'd best give some more attention to Jane. It will be time for rehearsal soon."

"Wait," Dolly put out a restraining hand. "I am sure you know it as well as you ever will. One of your great assets is your excellent memory. My dear, we've had little opportunity to talk of late and meanwhile, I see that this situation with Fearing is becoming increasingly serious. Are you sure it's what you crave?"

"He wants me," Thea said earnestly.

"Many others have—many others will. Especially after your London season."

"I am very fond of the Marquis," Thea assured her aunt.

"And what of Titus Croydon?"

"Titus Croydon!" Thea echoed indignantly. "Why do you mention him?"

"Because you do not. Yet I have noticed you are mighty edgy since you saw him. Could that be what has changed your mind?"

"Changed my mind?" Thea demanded. "What can you mean?"

"You were not nearly so encouraging to Fearing until he appeared."

Thea's eyes sparkled dangerously. "That has nothing to do with it."

"No?"

"No! Clive loves me. Titus never did. You—you know why he wed me."

"And having seen him again, how do you feel? Do you still maintain that you hate him?"

"More than ever. I . . . I loathe the very sight of him."

"Oh, dear, that's a pity."

"Do I not have reason?"

"Reason aplenty, but it would be far better if you merely disliked him. That's a much safer emotion than either hating or loathing."

"I do not understand you."

"Hatred implies deep feelings and those are often subject to change."

"Not mine."

"I hope not, but I should not make any rash promises to anyone—until I was completely sure."

"I am completely sure. I do not want to see him, ever again. And I can imagine that in the main, his sentiments are the same."

"That was not the impression I received from him. He seemed most anxious to see you."

"More curious than anxious, I should imagine," Thea said tartly. "Furthermore I am changed and that must pique his curiosity. However, I am sure that the main reason he wishes to see me is because he'd like to arrive at some decision concerning our marriage."

"You cannot blame him for that."

"I do not blame him, Aunt. I cannot imagine he wishes to remain tied to me any more than I to him. As I told you, Clive has suggested an annulment and I shall write to Titus as soon as I am finished with this engagement—but not before. I need to concentrate entirely upon the play and he must needs possess his soul in patience."

"You know, my dear," Dolly said. "I did not expect to like him, yet I found I did. I wonder . . ."

"Aunt Dolly," Thea said fiercely, "you are entitled to like whom you choose, certainly, but I pray you'll not continue to discuss him. I find the subject dreadfully boring." She rose, adding abruptly, "It is time to go to the theater."

Dolly guessed that a half hour must pass before it was time, but she decided it was more politic to remain silent, so she merely nodded and accompanied her niece out of the parlor.

There was something crawling on his chest. Titus Croydon, awakening from an uneasy sleep, made an exclamation of disgust and struck at the creature. "Good God," he muttered, "a roach."

"Aye, yer lordship, we got an 'ole population o' the critters'n even more o' lice. I 'ope yer lordship ain't too uncomfortable in this 'ere palace." A burst of ugly laughter followed this comment.

He did not answer. Indeed he was doubtful that he could have answered even if he had had that desire, which he did not. His throat was hoarse from shouting at the constable who had arrested him and at the magistrate who had ordered his detention, and at the turnkey, who had locked him in the cell, where he had already spent a wretched twelve hours—for he judged from the gray light filtering through the little square of window near the ceiling that it must be close on six in the morning.

If he were not in so precarious a position, he might have laughed at the irony of it, at the many ironies which had occurred since he had left London—was it only two mornings previously? However, at that moment, laughter was far from his lips. He was incarcerated in the Birmingham jail, suspected of impersonating and possibly robbing himself!

It was the final unlikely and frustrating occurrence in a series of similar episodes. They had begun with the discovery that Anthea was not on the coach to Birmingham, at least not on the one he had taken. The door had been firmly shut and the coach on the road before he had taken stock of his fellow passengers, learning, then, that there were two coaches to that destination, leaving within an hour of each other. He had been booked on the one which, after a stop in Birmingham, went on to Manchester. Obviously, Anthea had taken the other coach!

It had been a ghastly ride in that elderly and crowded vehicle. Two of the passengers had succumbed to its swaying motion and had been violently ill—fortunately out the window—but the sounds, the odor, and the spectacle had not been engaging. Another passenger, a small, wizened crone, seemed in utter fear of being robbed and was forever pawing through a basket, a sack, and a reticule, shrilly accusing those sitting next to her of harboring evil designs upon them. While he could not appreciate her tirades or her onion-scented breath or the occasional sharp jab of her bony elbow, Titus was glad that he had locked his money and other valuables securely into his trunk, then safely strapped to the top of the coach.

A little after five in the morning they had arrived at the Hotel Chalmers in Birmingham. Having had no sleep that night, he was half dead from fatigue. However, he had kept his wits about him. To avoid confusion over the luggage, he had registered as T. Manders. He smiled wryly as he recalled his valet saying, "But you cannot travel on a mail coach under your own name, my lord." He had agreed and, having compounded his lie on the hotel's register, he had followed the porter up to his room and fallen asleep the minute his head had hit the pillow. He had not awakened until one in the afternoon, only to learn that by some mischance his trunk had gone on to Manchester.

Another wry smile tugged at the corners of his mouth as he recalled that he had shrugged the matter off lightly enough and, having found a branch of the bank he used in London directly across the street, he had gone off to explain his position to its manager. As identification he had produced a letter which a fawning banker had assured him was proof enough. Instructing him to go back to his hotel and wait, he said he would send his cashier with the money. "Leave it with the clerk," Titus had instructed and had gone off to walk around the town—or more specifically to the Theater Royal, where, he had learned, a rehearsal was in progress and no one allowed to enter.

He had reached into his pocket for a half crown, only to discover that his pocket had been picked clean. Since he had been sitting near the window of the coach with only the elderly woman as his neighbor, he had no difficulty in ascertaining the identity of the thief. At the moment his annoyance had been mixed with amusement at the effrontery of one whom he had judged to be in her late seventies—even if her untoward actions had robbed him of the opportunity to view the rehearsal. He had strolled around to the front of the theater, where he had been further amused by the two busts ornamenting its facade—one being of Shakespeare and the other of Garrick. The actor, highly accomplished as he was said to be, hardly deserved to share a place beside the Bard. That he did pointed to the provincialism of the town.

A longer walk through its streets had strengthened that impression; there was little to be seen in the way of historical remains. The only point of real interest had been the canal where he had watched the men from the coal barges unload their inky cargoes. However, finding himself still weary from his hours on the road, he had made his way back to the hotel. He was about to inquire as to whether the cashier had left his money when the manager had feverishly rung a bell and a constable had popped out of the common room to accuse him loudly of being one Manders, posing as the Earl of Vane!

If he had been less tired, he might have handled the situation with tact rather than fury. From the distance of twelve long hours, he knew he had done everything to provoke and nothing to convince the law that he was, indeed, the Earl of Vane. In the days when he had called himself plain Titus Manders, he had been extremely circumspect in his dealings with those in authority. However, in his seven years of being an Earl, he had grown accustomed to preferential, even obsequious treatment by such underlings as constables and sheriffs. Accordingly he had been rude and highhanded with the Guardian of the Law— wrenching himself out of his hold and going as far as to strike the man, only to have two more of the fellows appear. They had laid rough hands on his person, blacking one of his eyes when he had continued to resist and at length dragging him unceremoniously to the court.

The presiding magistrate had refused to believe his furious explanation, maintaining that a belted Earl would hardly book passage on a mail coach. Nothing he could say had convinced the dullards of his true identity. And as his rage overcame his caution a second time, he was knocked down and dragged half-conscious to the jail, where, once he had regained his equilibrium, he had grasped the bars, repeating his assertion that he had been unlawfully detained and that he was the Earl of Vane. It had netted him only the raucous laughter and insults of his cellmates which numbered three—all ragged vagrants and two far gone on gin.

It had taken him some little time to calm himself, but by the time the lad who brought the bread and cheese allotted to each prisoner by the town authorities came, he had been able to discover that a single shilling remained in his other pocket. Presenting it to the boy, he begged him to take a message to Miss Thea Playfaire at the Theater Royal, informing her of his plight and begging her to come and identify him. He had waited impatiently, but hours had passed and the boy had not returned. Smarting from the blows inflicted upon him by the constable's men, he had been prey to the fear that the shilling had been pocketed and Anthea not approached—or had she been approached and refused to do anything about it? That, he had reasoned, was more than possible.

In the ensuing hours the jeers of his fellow inmates had brought him to a full realization of his predicament. What would happen if he could not convince his captors that he was the Earl of Vane? Would he be removed from this place which, he had discovered, was merely a lock-up house, and carried to prison? No, that was not possible. He could summon an advocate, but meanwhile there was no telling how long he must remain there—and all because of *her*. She had received his message. At length the boy had returned to tell him that he had left word at the theater. Obviously she, hating him with all the fury of a woman once scorned, was having her revenge upon him.

He glared up at the barred window. It had grown lighter and the sky was faintly blue. Horrible to see it from behind those bars.

"Belike they'll transport ye to Australy . . . that is if they don't 'ang ye for adoin' away wi' the Earl," the only sober one of his cellmates had jeered.

He had swallowed the hot words that had arisen to his lips. Of what use was it to protest that he was the Earl?

Now he put a hand to his chin and grimaced. It was bristly; his beard was heavy and grew fast. It was his custom to have his valet shave him twice a day. It was his custom to take at least two hot baths each day. It was his custom to change his linen as often as he thought it soiled. He drew in and exhaled a shuddering breath. His shirt was torn and soaked with sweat; his coat was filthied from lying upon it, for as the last to be locked into a cell that had only two cots, and these occupied by three men, he had slept on the floor and his body itched intolerably from the lice in the straw beneath him.

In another day or two he would be little more presentable than the drunken men beside him. It was a damnable situation and one which could, he now decided, be alleviated only if they would allow him to send word to his man of business to come and identify him. If only he had known someone else in this benighted town—someone besides an angry, bitter wife on whose account he had made this absurd journey, curse her. But she was not to be cursed. She was not to blame for what had happened. It was his own folly. She had a right to be angry and . . .

The sound of footsteps along the narrow walk that ran between the cells brought all speculation to a halt. A rattling of keys reached his ears. It was early, he thought, for the turnkey to make his rounds. However, any hope that he might be freed died aborning. If Anthea had wanted to secure his release, she would not have waited until the morning. Then he tensed. The footsteps had halted outside the cell door. The turnkey's face appeared in the small barred opening. "Is 'e wot calls 'isself the Earl 'ere?" he sneered.

Swallowing another angry rejoinder, Titus said, "Yes, I'm here."

Unlocking the door, the man ordered, "Come wi'me."

Rising stiffly and emerging into the passageway, Titus found that the turnkey was accompanied by two deputies holding pistols trained on the aperture. As the door was being closed, he heard his odious companion snigger, "G'bye, yer lordship. I 'ope to 'ave the pleasure of your grace's company again, I do."

Flanked by the two men, Titus was brought into a small office at the head of the corridor. His eyes widened. Facing him was the Marquis of Fearing. He regarded Titus without surprise. "Ah, good morning, Vane," he drawled.

Another man, whom Titus recognized as the jailer, stepped forward. "Is this individual truly the Earl of Vane?" he questioned sharply.

The Marquis eyed him in a manner that brought a dark flush to his cheeks before he responded. "I have so addressed him. That should be identification enough for you, my good fellow. I might add that you—the constable of this—er, village, as well as the officiating magistrate, if one can dignify him by such an appelation, have a great deal to answer for in their treatment of a peer of the realm."

The jailer paled and took a step backward. "I—I had nothing to do with it, your lordship. I—I only take orders. I . . ."

"Please, no more explanations. You begin to weary me," the Marquis interrupted. "I presume the Earl of Vane need no longer avail himself of your . . . er . . . hospitality?"

"No, of—of course, he . . . you m-may go, your lordship," the jailer favored Titus with an abject stare. "And b-believe me, your l-lordship, 'twas none o' my doing. I only . . ."

"Take orders," the Marquis finished. "Please—will you have your flunky unlock the necessary locks and show us the way out?"

It was only after they had left the confines of the jail that Titus found his voice. "I am grateful to you, Fearing," he croaked. "I expect my—Anthea told you of my situation?"

The Marquis nodded. "Yes, she was most concerned that she was unable to secure your release last night, but the dolts at the theater failed to deliver your message until it was too late to reach the proper individuals. Birmingham, alas, is not London." He stared at Titus. "It appears to me that you have sustained some rough usage. I hope you are not in pain?"

"It is nothing," Titus shrugged. "My lamentable temper . . ."

"I fancy that had I been in similar straits, my own temper must have been equally frayed. I understand that you came on the mail coach, arriving without luggage or funds?"

"Both were mistakenly conveyed to Manchester."

"Ah, just so," the Marquis's look was quizzical and it was obvious to Titus that several questions hovered on his tongue. Courtesy prevented him from voicing them. He continued, "I could let you have a change of clothing . . . we are much of a size. I could also provide you with monies."

"That will not be necessary, Fearing," Titus hastily assured him. He was finding it very difficult to express the gratitude he ought to feel. Instead he was wondering why the Marquis was in Birmingham. The answer his imagination was providing made it doubly hard for him to ask another favor but, unfortunately, it was necessary. He said, "If you would be good enough to identify me to the manager of my hotel, I am sure that will suffice. My bank can be informed and I shall be able to secure such funds as are needful."

"As you choose," the Marquis replied. "Let us be off."

"You are very kind," Titus managed to concede.

Since the hotel was not far from the jail, they went there on foot, covering the distance with a swiftness that pleased Titus. In spite of the Marquis's aid that morning, he was not at ease in his company, particularly since he cherished a growing suspicion that Fearing had divined the reason behind his odd decision to travel on a public conveyance. Yet, in spite of his innate distrust and dislike of the man, he could only admire his adroit handling of the hotel manager. After ceremoniously introducing his good friend Titus Croydon, Earl of Vane, he secured that embarrassed individual's stammering agreement that all who were concerned in what Fearing did not hesitate to describe as "this shabby affair" must subsequently be informed as to the true identity of his illustrious guest.

However, in bidding Titus farewell, Fearing confirmed his earlier suspicions by saying gently, " 'Tis a pity you decided to go by mail coach. We found the journey considerably shorter and certainly more comfortable by post chaise."

"Am I to take it that you accompanied Miss Playfaire to Birmingham?" Titus could not restrain himself from asking.

"Miss Playfaire *and* her aunt, yes," the Marquis nodded. "Will you attend the performance this evening? I should not miss it, if I were you. Jane Shore is one of her best roles. I have seen her play it more than once and each time I am amazed at her grasp of the character and her power to move an audience to tears." He bowed. "I shall bid you good morning, Vane."

It was even more difficult for Titus to reiterate his gratitude, but he managed it.

His first order on regaining his chamber was to have a bath and wash the grime and filth of the jail from his body. He had just finished donning his battered garments preparatory to seeing what he might find in the way of ready-made clothes to replace them, when there was a knock at the door.

"Well?" he called.

"If you please, your lordship," a porter opened the door a crack. "There be a female below wot wants to see ye."

"A female? Whom?"

"She be in the parlor, yer lordship."

"Her name . . . ," he began and stopped. Given his brief stay in Birmingham, there could be but one female who would come to see him. Moving out of his chamber so hastily that he nearly collided with the porter, he was down the stairs and into the parlor with a speed his mother would have understood.

He was breathing rather hard as he entered. He breathed the harder when he saw before him what he did not hesitate to term in his own mind a vision.

He had been correct about his visitor's identity. She was Miss Playfaire, as he supposed he must call her. She was all in blue, in a simple and elegant walking dress. Its lines were immensely flattering to her slender, graceful figure, its color equally kind to those incredibly blue eyes and to her shining hair. Her bonnet, a pale yellow straw, was high crowned and adorned with a ring of little blue daisies. In one blue-gloved hand she carried a frilly blue organdy sunshade and he noted that her little slippers were also blue.

He was conscious of a most surprising and alarming sensation in the region of his heart. Surely it was beating much faster than was its wont—for the look she gave him was soft and compassionate. Even as he opened his mouth to voice a warm greeting, he closed it again, as he recalled his earlier suspicions. They were enough to stifle his words, erase a burgeoning smile, and bring a frown to his eyes. "Good morning, Miss Playfaire," he said coolly.

Unaware of these manifestations of disapproval, Anthea regarded him anxiously. "Clive told me you were hurt." She moved a step nearer. "And yes, I see it. Your poor eye and your jaw so bruised. Your coat, too. Oh, I am so sorry that you were put through such an ordeal and for naught! I wanted to come with him this morning, but I fear I was sleeping when he left."

This ingenuous confirmation of his deepest suspicions brought Titus to a complete standstill. "You . . . were sleeping?" he repeated.

She betrayed her guilt by looking conscience-stricken. "Yes, I was so sorry. I had fully expected to come with him. Before I retired, I asked him to awaken me early in the morning, but he did not. We had such a late night, you understand. We were so occupied with . . ."

He raised a quelling hand. "Miss Playfaire, I pray you will not continue with these explanations which can only prove odious to me. I know the women of—of your profession have a franker speech than that employed in Polite Society and I know that many gentlemen are titilated by it. However, I myself am not of their number. Though it might prove surprising to you, I do not wish to hear any further details concerning your . . . connection with Fearing."

It was her turn to come to a standstill. She stared at him incredulously, the color slowly draining from her cheeks. "My c-connection with . . . with . . ."

He nodded, saying heavily, "It might interest you to know that I came to Birmingham in hopes that we might be taking the same coach. I wanted to talk to you. I also wanted to warn you that the noble Marquis of Fearing is hardly the company for a respectable female, but I see that I am too late."

The icy glitter that he had perceived in her eyes on the evening he had come to the greenroom at Drury Lane was back. Her tone matched it as she replied, "You are saying—"

"I am saying nothing more than that I wish you joy of your Protector and hope that your alliance will be of a longer duration than is usual with his affairs of the heart."

"Ah," she murmured. "I do thank you, sir. You are most magnanimous. I am quite sure that my—alliance must last at least longer than my previous connection with a noble lord. It is a great pity that you came all this way and suffered the embarrassment of being locked in jail—all for naught." Suddenly stepping to his side, she slapped him smartly across the cheek, adding fiercely "Were I a man, sir, I should call you out." Turning on her heel, she went swiftly from the room.

"Ah, that was ill done of you." Dolly Playfaire arose from a chair some distance away and came to confront Titus, who, in turn, looked back at her with considerable surprise. "Appearances," she continued, "are often deceiving and words do not always convey the meaning they are meant to present. I am very much afraid that you have wrought untold harm on my poor niece and possibly on yourself as well—for it does seem to me that you have her best interests at heart—whether or not you cherish a warmer regard for her.

"I must tell you that after a long, tiring rehearsal," she continued, "she spent the greater part of last evening knocking on doors and begging for a hearing that she might have you freed from what certain playwrights are fond of terming 'durance vile.' Her, er, Protector, as you most mistakenly called him, was unable to convince her that it were better to wait until morning. It was only with the greatest reluctance that she finally gave up her quest. I am really quite annoyed with you, Lord Vane. I do not think Fearing an ideal companion for Thea. However, he is much wiser than you. He knows exactly how to treat women or rather, the woman he wishes to impress." Upon concluding this extraordinary speech, she actually shook a finger at him before whisking herself out of the room.

Titus, staring at the door which she had closed none too gently, drew a long quavering breath. Pondering her words, he reached a most painful conclusion. "It is not true," he muttered out loud. But suddenly all the anguish and anger of the past two years seemed to take on a new dimension. He had always admitted to himself that he had been fond of the girl; now he could also admit that he might have entertained even a deeper feeling for her. He was not sure of that, but he was sure that he had made a most grievous error. A vision of her lovely face and her compassionate words came back to him. It was quite possible that his impulsive accusations had alienated her completely—and at a time when a little kindness, a little gratitude could have brought her to his side—and who could have told what might have happened then?

8

AT THE HOUR of eight in the evening, a hackney coach arriving before the building that housed Lord Vane's lodgings discharged a closely veiled female who paid off its driver with a trembling hand. Darting up the steps, she cast a terrified glance behind her. The coachman watched with a knowing smile. At night, such assignations formed the greater part of his trade and, more often than not, the ladies in question exhibited similar qualms. However, he thought, his smile broadening, these were never such as to impede them from reaching their destinations. As his imagination expanded, he climbed back into his seat, unwilling to dwell at length on the lurid images it presented. He had a night's driving ahead of him.

He would have been mightily disappointed had he been able to observe the meeting between the lady and the gentleman who admitted her into a suite of closed and shuttered rooms. The furniture was swathed in dust covers and the smell of camphor so heavy that she coughed and begged that a window be opened.

Upon performing that service, he greeted her without a trace of the rapture envisioned by the coachman. "You were able to obtain a description?"

"Yes," she spoke in a hushed voice—an unnecessary precaution since his servants were not in residence. "It was very difficult for me to come here," she added in a complaining tone. "I had to wait until Bertie was resting. If he were to learn of my absence . . ."

"No matter, I will set you down a few paces from your door within ten minutes . . . Now tell me what they will be wearing."

"She will be in a pale blue satin domino and matching mask. He will be clad in a black opera cloak with two shoulder capes. He'll also be wearing a black bicorne and, of course, a mask. Her wretched aunt will be in russet."

"Capital!"

"I hope it will prove helpful," she sighed.

"I cherish that same hope."

"It . . . it is shocking," she burst out. "That she should leave you and become a . . . a common actress!"

"Not a common actress, my dear Lady Heberdeen, a most uncommon one," he contradicted coldly. "I was able to see her as Jane Shore and can tell you that she is as expert in tragedy as she is in comedy."

She clicked her tongue. "You sound as if you were actually proud of her!"

"I cannot help but admire artistry."

"Artistry," she repeated. "That . . . artistry, as you are pleased to term it, will bring disgrace upon the lot of us, if she's at Drury Lane for the whole of next season. Others of her friends will certainly recognize her and the whole town will be alerted. It's a wonder it's not happened already, but fortunately none of those who saw her the night of Bertie's ball could have attended the play."

"Or if they did, they might not have known her. She is much changed."

"I cannot see that," she returned pettishly. "She is *older*, of course."

He resisted the temptation to give her a sharp answer. He was forced to depend upon her for news of Anthea, but he could not but regret that fact. The more he saw of little Lady Heberdeen, the more he disliked her. She might prate of scandal and notoriety, but he was sure that her main reason for appointing herself his ally was that she was riddled with jealousy and longed to make as much trouble for her sister-in-law as she could. It annoyed him that he was compelled to ask, "You will be there tomorrow night?"

"I have convinced Bertie that we must go."

"I am depending on you," he said. "I pray you'll not fail me."

"I swear I shall not. I do hope we are successful."

He did not like her use of the term "we," but since it was entirely applicable, he could only content himself with saying, "I will drive you back to Grosvenor Square, now."

"Ah," Dolly Playfaire unleashed a sentimental sigh. "It does seem an age since I was at Vauxhall Gardens for a masquerade." She raised her eyes heavenward, but she did not see the myriads of stars that flecked the sky. Instead she was looking at the vaulted ceiling of the colonnade enclosing the grand walk. "This"—she waved an arm at the painted iron pillars—"was not yet erected. Dear Michael would not have approved of it. He'd have thought it a shame that so many trees were cut down to make way for it. However, it is yet a pretty place. The roses are particularly beautiful, I think. And I must say that I am looking forward to the masquerade or—*ridotto*, if you prefer...I expect dear Bertie's already here."

"I expect he is," commented Anthea, "though I wonder if we should seek him out. Dorcas will not welcome my presence."

"Come, you are masked," the Marquis, who was walking at her side, smiled.

"A mask cannot render one invisible, Clive."

"Thanks be, else I should be robbed of the sight of you in that most becoming domino. Though it's a shame to hide your face, that part which remains is yet enchanting."

"La," Thea smiled up at him, "you'll turn my head."

"I would that were possible."

She laughed. "Shall we not make our way to the grove?"

"Yes," Dolly, hearing this snatch of conversation, nodded. "I can hear the orchestra. It sets my toes a-twitching and I am anxious to see the stand. I hear it's newly decorated and Theresa Kemble tells me there must be thousands of lights adorning it. She says it is amazing, an eighth wonder of the world."

"I fear Mrs. Kemble is easily amazed, ma'am," the Marquis drawled, "but come and you shall see whether or not you agree with her."

If it were not an eighth wonder of the world, the structure that housed the orchestra was yet a marvelously fanciful sight. Vaguely Oriental in design, its domed roof, topped by a glowing globe and encircled by slender spires, rose some fifty feet above the ground. Dome, spires, the fronts of a high ornamental balcony and of the lower platform which contained the orchestra were all encrusted with colored glass bulbs arranged in rows, in circles, and in swirls, their interior flames making them sparkle with a jewel-like radiance. Though sophisticates like the Marquis might comment that it looked like a French wedding cake, most visitors gaped in awe at the stand and certainly the flat wooden flooring that stretched before it was a fine spot for dancing. When the Marquis and his party arrived, a large group of maskers were whirling to the strains of a new German waltz.

The Marquis turned to Dolly, saying dutifully, "Might

I have this dance, ma'am?"

Her eyes glinted through the slits of the mask she had just donned as she responded, "Twenty years ago, my lord, I should have assented with pleasure, but now I should rather watch you waltz with Thea."

He bowed and, moving to Thea, held out his arms. She moved into them. It had been a long time since she had feared her clumsiness must discourage her partners. The grace that animated her body upon the stage did not desert her when she danced. As the Marquis guided her to the center of the floor, she found that he was given to complicated turns. She had no trouble following him, though, and if he held her a little closer than she ordinarily would have allowed, she could not protest for, as usual, she found herself invaded by the rhythm of the music. It was lovely to waltz with so expert a dancer, lovely, too, to look up and see the moon and the stars overhead. Her blissful mood was suddenly shattered by a woman's scream. Loud and piercing, it seemed to come from only a few feet away. She stopped abruptly, clutching the Marquis's arm. He tried to pull her aside but he was not in time to avoid another couple who burgeoned into them, backing away hastily with a spate of apologies. Several other couples had halted and were staring about them confusedly.

"I hope you are not shaken," the Marquis said anxiously.

"No, but what happened? It sounded as if she were being set upon by thieves . . ."

"More likely she was foxed," he returned unsympathetically. "Come, let us rejoin your aunt and wait for another waltz. But I charge you, stay close beside me. We must not get separated." Even as he uttered this injunction, a tall man in a black domino stumbled between them, falling against the Marquis and bearing him to the ground. It was some moments before Fearing could get himself untangled. "Blast you," he shouted. "Could you not watch where you were going?"

Evidently affrighted by this reprimand, the man mum-

bled something unintelligible and hurried away. Rising, the
Marquis looked for Thea and saw the glint of her blue satin
cloak several paces ahead of him. He hurried to catch up
with her. "I am sorry, but why did you not stay where you
were. I told you we must not be separated, Thea."

A giggle met his ears and an entirely different voice said,
"But I am not Thea."

He looked at her in consternation, seeing now that a
ginger-hued lock of hair had strayed from beneath her hood.

"I beg pardon, ma'am . . . a mistake."

"Oh, that be all right," she put her hand on his arm.
"I don't mind sayin' I shouldn't mind if I was this Thea.
You look a proper sort to me."

He did not trouble to reply. Moving away from her, he
saw that somehow he had become turned around and was
on the other side of the floor. Scanning the mass of people
before him, he looked for another pale blue satin domino
but no such sight met his troubled gaze.

Meanwhile, Thea, pulled away from the Marquis's side
by the man who had stumbled against him, had been thrust
into the middle of the milling crowds. Looking for Clive,
she had a moment of panic as she did not see him—but
then, he joined her, setting his bicorne right and then holding a handkerchief to his mouth. "Ah, here you are, my
dear," he said in a muffled voice. "I pray you, let us get
away before we meet with further harm."

"Were you much hurt?" she demanded anxiously.

"I'll not die from it, but there's dust in my throat," he
coughed again.

"You must have some wine," she said.

He nodded and, putting his arm lightly around her waist,
he expertly shepherded her out of the crowds and toward
one of the little colored tents where refreshments were sold.
Yet, as they neared it, he groaned and veered away. "Let
us sit there." He pointed to a small bower. "My knee—I
must have injured it when I fell."

"Oh, not badly, I hope?"

"I did not think so, but 'tis aching," he said as he peered into the bower only to be greeted by a titter and a sharp "Be off wi' ye." He moved back hastily with another cough, saying ruefully, "It's occupied, but there's another further along that walk." He limped in that direction.

"Oh, you did hurt yourself!" she exclaimed distressed. "What a pity that man was so clumsy. I hope we may find a place to sit down soon."

"There do you not see it."

"But that is some distance away. Should you like to lean on me, Clive, dear."

"No." He coughed once more and cleared his throat. "'Tis not necessary . . . though you are kind, Thea."

In another moment they had reached a miniature folly furnished with benches and a table. Over it was a lattice hung with flowering vines which trailed over the entrance, helping to hide it from prying eyes. Little lamps similar to those which had decorated the orchestra stand gleamed amidst the surrounding trees and a small, dim lantern hung inside the folly.

It was not until she had aided the limping Marquis to a bench that Thea became aware of the dimness of the interior and of the sequestered location of their haven. She flushed, remembering the giggle that had issued from the other bower. "I—hope you will feel better presently," she said. "My aunt must be wondering where we have gone." She raised her eyes to his face and found it shadowed by his hat. She wished he were not masked. It gave him, she thought, an oddly unfamiliar and even a sinister look.

"I hope that you are not afraid of me, my dear."

His prescience startled her. "No, of course not," she hastened to assure him.

"Then, I beg you will sit down." He indicated the other bench.

She obeyed. "Does your knee still pain you?"

He rubbed the limb. "Not grievously, but I should like to remain here a bit longer. Still if you wish to go . . ."

"Why should you think that I do, Clive?"

"You seem uncommon nervous. Or am I mistaken?"

"I am not nervous." She smiled. "I know I can trust you."

"Of course, you can. It is pleasant here in the dark. Can you smell the roses?"

"No," she said after an experimental sniff, "actually I do not."

"No? Perhaps it is your scent that fills my nostrils," he said softly.

"I do not know." She tried to speak lightly and was annoyed to hear a little tremor in her voice. It was ridiculous, she thought angrily, to be wary of Clive. She was acting like the veriest schoolgirl. Yet there was something different about him tonight. Even when she had been locked in his embrace, she had not been so aware of his presence. Though a table stood between them, it seemed as if he were all around her. She tried to shrug the feeling away but it persisted. She could not understand it. Then, she tensed. She had let one arm lie across the table and now he had clasped it lightly—but light as that touch was, it generated an excitement he had never roused in her before. She thought she should pull away, but such a move would be ridiculous. She, who had submitted to his kisses, could scarcely protest so mild a familiarity. It would only hurt his feelings.

"You are very taut, my dear," he coughed. "I think that in spite of all you've said, you are afraid of me."

"Of course I am not, Clive," she managed a slight laugh. "Still if you are feeling more the thing, should we not return. You ought to have some wine or water. Your voice is quite hoarse."

"My knee still throbs but . . ." Clutching the table, he endeavored to rise.

"Oh, no, please. I can see you are in pain," she put out a protesting hand.

Seizing it, he kissed it. "You are very kind."

"I am s-sorry you s-sustained such a fall." Her hand was actually tingling from the touch of his lips. She did not understand herself, not at all.

"I am not sorry, now. It is very pleasant being with you, though I wish I might see your face."

"The witching hour's not yet come."

"But it has . . . the witching hour is any hour I spend with you." He reached for her hand again, caressing her palm. She shivered. "Are you cold?" he inquired.

"No, not in the . . . the least. It's passing warm tonight, but—"

He released her hand and she felt as if a great weight had fallen from her. But, at the same time, she was sorry that it was gone. Then she gasped out an indignant protest, for he had suddenly pulled her mask off.

"Come, what harm can it do for me to look upon your face, my dear?"

"But it is . . . it is . . ."

"Forbidden like the fruits that hang upon the trees in Paradise?"

"You are in an odd mood tonight, Clive."

"Odd? Do you find me . . . odd?"

"Yes. Please, I wish you'd give me my mask."

"No."

"You . . . I cannot think what has happened to you, Clive."

"*You* have happened to me."

She rose, chiding, "I must ask you to remember that I am not free."

"How can I not remember that." He rose, too, his tall form blocking the entrance. "But must we remember it tonight?"

"More than ever—tonight." She tried to laugh. "Now come, we must return to the grove. I am sure you are more comfortable now."

"On the contrary, I have never been in greater need of comfort." Putting his arms around her, he drew her into his embrace.

"Clive, I pray you." Her protests were stifled by his kiss. Determinedly she struggled, but his arms were viselike. She did not want to return the pressure of his lips nor open her mouth to receive his tongue, but she could not withstand its probing. Shivering with an excitement she had felt only once before, she surrendered with parted lips. It occurred to her in some still-conscious part of her mind that those who were lightning-struck must feel some similar fiery shock.

It seemed to her that he felt it, too. It seemed to her that they were igniting each other. His hands were traveling down her body—caressing her, practiced caresses which aroused throbbing pulses. She wanted to remain pressed against him, she wanted to feel his body melding into hers, as once long ago—but it was wrong. He had no right to take advantage of her. Half sobbing, she struggled to be free of him. "Let me go . . . I pray you, let me go," she cried.

He moved back from her and his answer came loud, clear, bereft of either cough or hoarseness, "I'll never let you go, Anthea. Tell that to your precious Clive—and let him pursue some other man's wife."

She went limp with shock. "T-Titus."

"Your very obedient servant, my love."

"Oh!" She put both hands on his chest, pushing him away from her furiously. "Release me at once." His arms fell away so quickly that she stumbled. She felt strangely cold, no not cold, hot and angry and confused but uppermost among her emotions at that moment was astonishment. "How . . . how is it possible?"

He removed his mask. "This made it entirely possible."

"But I . . . I—where is Clive?"

"I imagine he is wondering much the same about you."

"But how . . . ?"

" 'Twas easy, but no matter. You asked me for an annulment. I have understood these may be obtained only when the marriage was not consummated."

"I . . . I will not discuss it with you now," she cried. "Of all the shabby tricks . . ."

"I agree, but I had no other choice. You'd not see me again in Birmingham. I sent letters to you at the Theater Royal; the manager returned them to me torn in half. I sent letters to Drury Lane and since they went unacknowledged, I imagine they met much the same fate. Consequently I had no choice but to resort to trickery. I did not like taking such unfair advantage of you, but I cannot now say that I am sorry I did. You are a sweet armful, my own."

"You . . . you . . ." She found herself with so many angry words piled upon her tongue that she was unable to express any of them.

"I expect this annulment is by way of retaliation."

"Retaliation? I do not understand you, my lord."

"I refer to our last unfortunate encounter for which I am truly sorry. Suffice to say I was not myself then. A night in jail is not the best way to begin a morning. I do not believe he is your Protector."

"I do not care what you believe."

"I am most penitent for everything I said to you. If you'd troubled to read my letters, you'd know that."

"You might have spared yourself the writing of them, my lord."

"If that annulment was not by way of retaliation, why did you not propose it two years ago?"

"I . . . I had not thought it could be implemented and I . . . did not wish to see you. I was not thinking clearly."

"Indeed, you could not have been, else you would not have left me in that precipitate manner."

"I merely based my behavior on your own."

He paused. "I am sorry for that but—"

"You need not apologize to me now."

"If you'd given me a chance to explain . . ."

"What might you have said? That, like a good dutiful son, you obeyed your mother?"

Anger pulsated through his tones. "If you knew me better," he intoned coldly, "you'd know that I was never in thrall to my mother. If I'd not found you delightful, if I'd not liked you as much as I did, nothing she could have said would have moved me to wed you. You found me in the library that night, did you not? I must tell you that I had decided not to go into the ballroom. I had promised my mother I'd come to your ball, but I'd not promised her I'd meet you. I know that's a fine line of distinction, but I was preparing to draw it when you came in. Meeting you, I thought we might deal well together."

"And changed your mind as soon as our wedding night?"

"No, I . . . I cannot," he broke off. "I . . ."

"I beg you'll not cudgel your brain for excuses. Your actions spoke louder than any words."

"If you'd been patient . . ."

"Patient, or submissive? If I'd remained and provided you with the heir you coveted, would you have then patted me on the back and said, 'Thank you, good cow?'"

"Anthea . . ."

"Thea," she corrected sharply. "Thea Playfaire. Anthea, sweet, docile, pliable, believing, stupid, stupid, *stupid*, Anthea is no more. Consider her deceased!"

"You are yet Anthea Croydon. We have exchanged marriage vows. These are binding ties."

"I do not recognize those ties, which brings us back to the annulment, which I desire you not to contest!"

"An annulment will not serve."

"I was with you only three days. Or rather I was at Vane for three days."

"My beautiful Thea, no one seeing you would believe that a man who calls himself a man, would have you and

not act the man with you. My dear, make the best of it.
Stay with me. I can make you happy—happier than Fearing
ever could. Surely I have proved that tonight." He reached
for her again.

She stepped back, glaring at him. He had sounded so
self-confident, so sure that she would gladly fall into his
arms—after all that had happened. He had no right to be
so sure of her. Furiously she retorted, "I do not believe
that . . . not for an instant. Two people who do not love
each other cannot be bound together like—like prisoners.
I have given my word to Clive and I shall keep it."

"You could not give that word, you gave it to me. You
are mine," he said in a low, pained voice. "And I mean
what I say—I shall never let you go."

"We'll see about that," she retorted. He had moved a
little to one side and she, perceiving a slight opening, darted
through it and ran across the path into the shrubbery.

He was after her in a moment. "Anthea, Anthea," he
called loudly. "Come back . . . I pray you."

Slipping under the overhanging branches of a fir tree,
she lay quietly, scarcely daring to breathe.

He continued to call her name and she heard him crashing
through the undergrowth. She lay there for a full ten minutes
while his voice sounded fainter. Then she crawled out and,
making her way from tree to tree along the path to the
grove, she finally reached it.

Brushing leaves and dirt off her cloak, she stepped into
the light and immediately heard her name called. The Marquis hurried to her side. "Where have you been?" he asked
anxiously.

"I—" It was on the tip of her tongue to tell him about
Titus's outrageous actions, but even as the words came to
her lips, she swallowed them. To tell Clive the truth would
only provoke him to fury. Undoubtedly he would call Titus
out and Titus was a master swordsman! For his sake, *Clive's*
sake, there must be no duel. "Somehow I got carried along

by the crowds. I thought you right behind me and I started up one of those paths . . . and I became hopelessly lost. Where is Aunt Dolly?"

"She, too, has been searching for you." He put an arm around her. "We were both afraid you might have met with some misadventure." He stared at her. "Your mask . . . why did you remove it. That was not very wise."

"I could not see where I was going."

He gave her a long look. "Are you telling me the whole truth, Thea?" he asked suspiciously.

She gave him an affronted stare. "Why would I lie to you?" she countered.

"You seem very much on edge."

It occurred to her that she was weary of having her emotions diagnosed by other people. However, she said, "I had difficulty getting back here and I was worried about not finding you."

"My dear," Dolly hurried up to them. "Oh, I am so glad to see you. I had fears of you're being spirited away by one of those masked bandits, for that, I vow, is what half of them are. I have stopped counting how many times I have been accosted. Where were you, Thea?"

"I was lost."

"That can be a most distressing experience."

"It was. I should like to go home." She looked pleadingly at the Marquis. "Should you mind, Clive?"

"No, not in the least. I cannot think that we have been very well entertained, this evening."

"No . . . and the whole character of the gardens has changed since last I was here," Dolly agreed.

The Marquis slipped an arm around Thea's waist. "Come, then, my love," he murmured.

She waited in vain for the excitement that Titus had engendered with that same gesture. It was not forthcoming, but it did not matter. She respected Clive. He would never have let his mother order his life or force him to marry when he did not choose to do so. And if Titus did not grant the annulment, there was another way of freeing herself. She did not care for that alternative, but under the circumstances, she had no choice—unless she wanted to remain with Titus, which she did not and would not!

9

THE PARLORMAID WHO ushered Thea Playfaire into the library of Heberdeen House was young and impressionable. Assuring her that her brother would be informed of her arrival immediately, she passed the word to a footman, who in turn carried it to Sir Bertram's valet. Meanwhile she hurried to the servant's hall where Lady Heberdeen's abigail was having a cup of tea. Generally this personage was far too top lofty to speak with a mere parlormaid, but since they were alone in the chamber, she condescended to hear a breathless description of the visitor.

"I never seen 'er look so beautiful . . . all in lavender, she were an' a love o' a bonnet an' a silk sunshade wi' a long ivory 'andle an' lavender kid gloves an' . . ."

"That's nothing out of the ordinary," said the abigail. "But what brought her here at such an hour?"

"She didn't inform me as to that, but I can tell you she were in a rare takin'. You should've seen 'er eyes. Oh, wouldn't I gi' a pony to 'ear wot she'll be sayin' to 'im."

"You should have listened at the door."

This remark was delivered in a most sarcastic tone of voice but its implication was lost on the parlormaid. "I couldn't," she replied regretfully. "Bob is still dustin' the 'all."

"A pity." The abigail set down her cup. "I'd best see to Milady's tea." Though she walked from the chamber in the slow dignified manner that befitted one of superior status, her movements, once she had gained the corridor, were surprisingly speedy.

In the library Thea, pacing up and down, was suddenly arrested by the sight of the Queen Anne chair and all at once, the room, bathed in early sunshine, seemed to darken. In her mind's eye, she saw a plumpish girl in white standing against the door. In her mind's ear was that amused voice asking her if she were pursued by a dragon. She also envisioned a shadowy form rising from the chair. She banished this ghost. She would not let it approach her. How cozened she had been by his appearance and his manner. He had seemed so masterful, so strong—and all the while he had been a puppet, worked by strings held in the hands of his mother. That was the truth, no matter how he tried to deny it! And was his mother's hand to rule her life forever?

"Anthea."

She turned to find her brother limping in. He was wearing a long brocade robe. It, too, brought back unwelcome memories. It was similar in design and even color to that which he had worn when he had come into her room on their wedding morning, when he had reaffirmed his love for her. But there was a difference—the air of happiness was gone. There were new lines about his mouth, lines which told of bitterness, and his eyes were disillusioned. Her hopes had not been realized, but her fears had. His marriage had failed to bring him the comfort he had expected.

"Oh, Bertie," she sighed and held out her hands.

He held them warmly. "My dear, what is amiss?"

In a low voice she replied, "I wanted you to know that I am about to start an action for divorce."

His grip tightened convulsively. "Divorce?" he repeated loudly. "But, Anthea, have you given this your full consideration?"

"I have," she said defiantly. "And I have discussed it with Clive."

"And he is in agreement?"

"He is not pleased about it, but yes, he agrees with me that there is no other way. Titus will not countenance an annulment. He is being altogether outrageous and cruel and spiteful and . . ."

"Hold, love," Bertie looked at her gravely. "Have you considered that his attitude springs from the fact that he still cares for you?"

"No, because he does not. He never cared for me. 'Tis but his pride that's hurt. He'd not like to see himself bested by Fearing."

"But, my dearest, if you are divorced, you must know what that will mean. You'll never be able to enter the Polite World again."

"That world is no longer my world. I am an outcast, a stage actress, a vagabond."

"Hush," he said sternly. "You could return if you wished, yes, at this very moment—but not if you are divorced. You'd never be received. You'd need to go and live upon the Continent. Would Fearing be willing to accompany you?"

"He swears he will live with me anywhere," she returned. "He loves me."

"Are you sure of him?"

"I . . . yes, I am sure. He has promised to stand by me. I know that no one else will. If you do not wish to see me again, I will quite understand."

"My dear, dear love, I would wish to see you under any

circumstances. You will always be welcome in my house
but since Titus is willing, could you not try and . . ."

"No, I beg you'll say no more," she cried hotly. "I love
Clive. I want to be with him. I am determined on it. I will
never change my mind. Clive will be taking me to his
advocate tomorrow. He will instruct him to begin proceed
ings."

Having snatched a cup of tea and drunk it so hastily that
her throat still burned from its passing, the parlormaid had
returned to work, her dusting taking her in the direction of
the library. As she neared that interesting portal, she came
to a dismayed halt. Lady Heberdeen, clad in a peignoir, her
hair falling about her shoulders and still tousled from the
night, stood close to it.

The girl backed away hastily, hoping that she had not
been seen. She was reasonably sure that Lady Heberdeen
would have dealt very harshly with anyone of the household
who might have seen her at that moment. Once the maid
was safely back in the drawing room, she dared to giggle
at the thought of the mistress listening at the door just as
if she had been a prying servant herself! That was why she
had been there; she would have laid a shilling on it and
stood to collect, too!

The Marquis of Fearing, tooling his curricle expertly
through the crowded purlieus of Charles Street, brought his
chestnuts to a halt. Signaling Moses to take the ribbons,
he alighted. Directly across the street was the building
where Titus Croydon's lodgings were located. He frowned
at its massive door. It was upon impulse that he had come
at this early hour of the morning, but he had no desire to
confer with Croydon, nor could he believe he would receive
a favorable answer to his plea, but he had to make the
attempt. Yet, would it not be a waste of time? The letter
Thea had received had made Vane's stand quite clear. He

could not for conscience's sake agree to an annulment.

"Conscience," he scoffed.

"Beggin' yer pardon, sor," Moses looked at him questioningly. "Wot did ye ask me?"

"Nothing, lad," he said hastily. He had not been aware that he had spoken out loud. It was not his way save when he was disturbed—and he was extremely disturbed. The idea of a divorce was entirely repugnant to him. He had known only one other couple in his immediate circle who had wed with such a shadow hanging over them. They had removed to Paris, where, in a very short time, they had quarreled and gone their separate ways—he returning to London and she retiring to Venice, where, it was said, she lived a life of depravity.

While he could not imagine himself leaving Thea, the idea of being estranged from his friends and, worse, infinitely worse, his son, was terrible to him. He heaved a long and bitter sigh. When he had first met Thea, he had wanted only to make her his mistress, and then he had discovered that she was a Heberdeen. One could not cast a Heberdeen in such a role—not even a theatrical Heberdeen, and that was his only alternative. He shook his head. There was another choice. He might leave her, but he could not. There had been moments when he had questioned the depth of his love for her, but to be in her presence a moment was to have those questions answered in strong affirmatives. No woman, he was sure of that, had ever fascinated him half so much, and the idea of possessing her utterly was one that, in turn, possessed him, rendering him weak with desire and filling his nights with the most explicit and uncomfortable dreams.

He had to have her and he could not have her without marriage. Damn Croydon for a damned cur in the manger, he thought furiously, wishing he had a reason for calling him out and running a sword or firing a pistol through his heart—but one could not challenge a man for refusing to

grant an annulment! Right was on his side. The marriage
had been consummated. He had broken Thea's heart and
he, Clive Alacorn, had been able to mend it and Croydon
did not have the decency, the honor . . .

A dray and several carriages rumbled past him. As they
vanished in the distance, he saw that a post chaise had
drawn up in front of the building across from him. Then
he bit down an exclamation of surprised annoyance as Croydon emerged from the door of the mansion with a heavily
veiled woman. She was very tiny and her outlines were
vaguely familiar. He had a sense of having seen her before,
of knowing her, but he could not place her. Croydon was
assisting her into the waiting vehicle and a postillion had
dismounted to strap luggage on its roof.

He frowned. Croydon was obviously leaving town—and
with a woman, damn him. His mistress? Undoubtedly. She
had been fashionably gowned, probably with his money.
Fearing, whose purse had been at the disposal of many a
lady fair, could not fault him for that nor for having a
mistress at the very moment when he was trying to persuade
his wife to return to him. One had nothing to do with the
other, but it was insufferable that he should leave town with
her—on a pleasure trip, when so much needed to be settled!
He would have given a good deal to have intercepted him,
but as a gentleman he could not. Cursing the code of ethics
that he must needs obey, he could only stand and watch as
the coachman flicked the whip over the backs of four beautifully matched grays. With the postillion mounted on one
of them, the post chaise joined the street traffic and was
soon lost to sight.

Toward five in the afternoon of that same day, the Marquis brought his curricle to a stop outside Dolly Playfaire's
cottage in Islington. Five hours of tooling up and down the
roads just outside the city, brooding on the situation and
Titus Croydon, whom he heartily wished at the bottom of
the Thames, had not improved his temper. He had not told

Thea of his errand that morning, but he had hoped against hope to bring her news of a *fait accompli*. As it was, they could speak only of divorce. It was with a heavy heart and heavy tread that he went slowly up the steps. The door opened very quickly to his knock, as if the maid, who admitted him, had been stationed behind it for that very purpose. He noted that her eyes were reddened as if she had been weeping and that her cap was awry. That surprised him. Dolly's servants were always neat.

He was due for another surprise, when, upon being ushered into the parlor, he found Dolly standing in the middle of it, looking more like a tragedy queen than the toast of the comedy stage. She was actually wringing her little hands. Her greeting further confounded him. "Ah, at last you have come," she cried accusingly. "I was afraid my messages must have miscarried."

"Your messages?" he repeated blankly.

"You did not receive them, then?"

"I have not been home." His heart smote him. "Has something untoward happened . . . Thea . . . ?"

"Yes, she—she has gone—been taken, I should say."

"Taken," he echoed. "You are surely not telling me that she has been abducted?"

"Yes, yes, yes, that is what I am telling you. I can think of no other explanation. Oh, it passes all bounds of understanding. It is a proceeding so thoroughly reprehensible that I can scarce credit it."

It was a moment before he could say, albeit chokingly, "I pray you'll tell me about it, ma'am." He never knew what moved him to add with an awful certainty, "'Twas Croydon, no doubt?"

Her round green eyes grew rounder and actually seemed to shoot forth little sparks. "Yes, the same," she cried. "How could you know? Did he . . ."

"No, no," he said hastily. "It was a guess. Tell me what happened!"

Motioning him to sit down, she sought her sofa but
bounced up in a trice, pacing back and forth as she went
on to explain in anger-edged accents how a message had
come from Titus Croydon advising Thea that he would wait
upon her at the hour of eleven to discuss the framing of
annulment papers. He had arrived in his post chaise. He
had been most polite and agreeable, explaining that he had
rethought the matter and had decided that this was far the
better course. He had asked if she would come with him
to put her signature to certain documents. Naturally she had
assented joyfully and gone, taking with her her abigail.
"And that," Dolly concluded, "was six hours since. I sent
a message to his lodgings and my man came back to tell
me that . . ."

"He had gone," the Marquis said in a hard tone.

"Yes! Oh, it passes all understanding and she, poor child,
so happy that she need not start proceedings for that horrid
divorce. Indeed she came back from her brother's house
this morning in tears—though she might have expected his
reaction. Of course he was kind for, as you know, he loves
her dearly, but he felt it his duty to point up the exigencies
of a life lived in the shadows, as it were. Though he did
agree that under the circumstances she had no alternative."

"Hold, ma'am," he interrupted, "am I to understand that
Thea was at Bertie's house this morning? Before she received the message from Croydon?"

"Yes, she went practically at the crack of dawn and
returned no later than eight."

"And Croydon's message . . . when did it arrive?"

"I should say that it came about thirty minutes past the
hour of ten."

His eyes narrowed. "Had Croydon been informed of
Thea's intentions concerning the divorce?" he asked.

"No, of course not. None knew save Bertie and he would
not have told . . ."

"What about Lady Heberdeen?" the Marquis asked in

a hard voice. "He must have told her."

"No," Dolly said slowly. "I do not think he would. It would be an intelligence that must shock her and . . ." She paused, openmouthed, as he strode to the door. "You are going?"

"Yes, there's one I must see."

"But, my lord," she began indignantly and closed her mouth for she was addressing the empty air.

It was with fury welling in his heart and a prayer, or rather an incantation, running through his mind that the Marquis of Fearing set his foot upon the marble steps of Heberdeen House. Negotiating them in two bounds, he slammed the knocker against it's brass plate with a clang that must have sent reverberations throughout the entire house. It was with considerable difficulty that he managed to control his rage as he faced the startled butler who appeared on the threshold.

Recognizing him, the man said, "Please come in, my lord."

Striding into the hall, the Marquis rasped, "Is Lady Heberdeen at home?" Then, before the man could answer, Fearing looked beyond him to see the tiny figure that had caught his eye earlier that day—the only difference being that she was not veiled. His prayer had been most fortuitously answered!

She gave him an uncertain smile. "You wished to see me, my lord?"

Striding to her side, he stared down at her furiously. "Where is she? Where has Croydon taken her?"

Dorcas took a faltering step backward. "I . . . I do not know who—or what you are talking about."

He had an impulse to shake her until her teeth rattled. However, since it would serve no purpose, he said as calmly as he could, "I think, Lady Heberdeen, that you know exactly what I am talking about and I want the truth from you. It might interest you to know that I saw you this morning with Croydon, coming forth from his lodgings at a very early hour. If you were not there upon an assignation . . ."

Her bosom swelled and she drew herself up, retorting, "How dare you! As if I, a respectable married female would lend myself to . . . to . . ."

"Clive, might I have an explanation of what you have just said to my wife?"

Emitting a little scream, Dorcas backed away from Sir Bertram, who stood on the threshold of the small chamber leading off from the hall. "B-Bertie," she mouthed. "Oh, I pray you, this terrible man . . ."

The Marquis cut across her gabbled protests and turning to Sir Bertram, he said, "Yes, you may have an explanation, Bertie. I presume you are aware that your sister has been abducted, though you might not be aware that this . . . woman might very well have had a hand in it. And if she does not tell me the whole of what she knows . . ."

"What I know! I know nothing, nothing," Dorcas cried. "You must not believe him, Bertie. He could not have s-seen me." Her hand stole to her mouth and tottering backward, she fell carefully to the floor in an approximation of a swoon.

There was a bowl of roses on a nearby table and with a speed astonishing for a man so incapacitated, her husband possessed himself of it. Throwing its contents upon the face of his recumbent spouse, he said icily, "My dear, you are not near so accomplished an actress as my sister. Now, I charge you, inform us as to your role in these reprehensible proceedings, or by heaven, I will beat it out of you."

Twilight was turning into darkness and in his corner of his post chaise Titus, holding up a scratched hand and a bitten finger, broke a long silence by saying conversationally, "I imagine that the first Baron of Vane must have suffered similar wounds when he took the Lady Beatricia away from her wedding party." He touched the side of his face, which was embellished by a long red scratch. "It did not," he continued, "deter the Baron from imprisoning her in his Keep. In lieu of a Keep, ours being ruined, as you no doubt remember, I am taking you to my grandfather's hunting box in Leicestershire. It is just beyond the village of Melton Mobray, where the Quorn, Cottsmore, and Belvoir Hunts meet. I am not fond of fox hunting. I think it cruel. I do not care to kill deer, either. Though venison is tasty, my soul delights in seeing the creatures as they leap through the forest. Have you ever seen a leaping deer? I am not familiar with the land around The Corners, but I am sure there must be deer in the park. 'Tis a most graceful sight. However, my grandfather, my father, and my brother Odo were not of the same mind, and you'll see the antlers and the heads of their various quarries in the main hall, the drawing room, the dining room, and the library. The hunting box, while not large—twenty rooms only, I believe, is much more comfortable than the Keep must have been. The chamber in which the Lady Beatricia was imprisoned was large but also draughty and I am sure the fireplace smoked, there being no really adequate chimney. Life in those days was much simpler. They had not heard of divorce. They adhered to the Bible. 'Therefore shall a man leave his father and his mother, and shall cleave unto his wife; and they shall be *one* flesh . . .'"

A sniff interrupted this discourse. The sound did not come from the trussed and gagged figure in the other corner but from Sally Plant, her abigail, huddled in the seat facing them and quite rigid with terror, having not dared to struggle as had her mistress when she had discovered that the post chaise rather than taking her to the heart of the city was on the road leading out of it.

Looking at her, Titus said, "Come, girl, do not sniffle. You are in no danger, neither of you."

"Oh, sor," sobbed Sally, "I dasn't know . . . I really dasn't know . . ." Upon this ambiguous utterance, she lapsed once more into a stricken silence.

"Though that remark could refer to any one of a number of things about which you are ignorant, let me tell you that since we have been on the road upward of eight hours, we shall soon arrive at our destination. I regret the necessity of keeping you both in this post chaise for such a long time, but to have brought you into the Scarlet Crown, where we changed horses, would have been difficult. I could not have gagged nor bound my wife and undoubtedly she would have leveled embarrassing accusations at me, which might have been credited. Beauty in Distress can always be sure of a large and gallant audience. I am afraid, my good girl, that I did not trust you not to make an outcry, either. However, we should be at Renard Manor, named as you might guess for a fox, albeit of French origin, in a little less than an hour."

"It be gettin' so dark," moaned the abigail.

"I cannot deny it."

"An' there be 'ighwayman about."

A stifled sound from Thea netted her Titus's instant attention. "I expect your mistress would say—had she the use of her tongue—that you are in the company of an 'ighwayman, at this moment. I might mention that my men are equipped with the necessary firearms and I think you will sustain no harm from such professional footpads, cutthroats, and other rogues as abound in these parts." Having so spoken, he fell back into the silence that he had maintained almost from the moment of leaving London.

Thea's wrists, bound together with strong twine, lay in her lap. They felt numb, as did her ankles which were similarly fettered. Though the gag was not tight enough to cause great discomfort, the fact that she could not express all the sentiments that had been whirling in her head for the hours she had not spent in an uneasy doze, was particularly infuriating. Since some of these were questions concerning their ultimate destination, her curiosity in that regard had, at least, been satisfied. However, other questions remained. How long would she be kept there? She reasoned drearily that she might remain in his custody for weeks, months, even years, for no one knew of their destination. Meanwhile she would be at the mercy of this villainous, vile, vicious—no, he was not vicious, but his actions were execrable, damnable, disgraceful, scandalous, and redolent of the greatest impropriety! And had she the use of her tongue, he would have received the full force of it. Her bosom heaved as she thought of the snare he had laid for her.

No one could have been more polite, more reasonable than he as he had escorted her from Dolly's cottage to his waiting post chaise. She had, she recalled bitterly, marked the luggage strapped to it and questioned him about it. He had explained that he was due to make a short visit to Vane—at his Mother's urgent request which, of course, he dared not ignore. Moreover he had assured her that he would be back in London within two days to participate in plans to speed the annulment.

Thea ground her teeth. Lies, lies, lies! And she had actually thanked him for his capitulation.

Then, to look out the window and find that they were on the high road! She had actually dared to try and open the door, at which time he had restrained her. She had struggled, fought, and bit, but she had not realized he was so strong. He had subdued her with an ease she found particularly demeaning, the while her abigail had fluttered about like a frightened moth, or rather bird, since moths were silent and the wretched girl was full of little helpless moans like a scared owl, if owls were ever scared. She did not know much about owls and why was she even dwelling on them? She must be growing light-headed from lack of sustenance—she had refused the cold meat and tea he had offered. Then, suddenly, something he had said caused her to stiffen and pale.

He had mentioned divorce and how had he known of it? She had not yet penned the letter informing him of her intention. Only one other person beside herself, her aunt, and Clive knew what she was contemplating and that was Bertie. Had he informed Titus as to her decision? She could not believe that. How had he found out? How had he found out that she would be at Vauxhall Gardens—and he must have known what she would wear. Her brother had known, too. Her eyes narrowed; her brother and his *wife*. Was Dorcas the informant? It was quite possible. It was entirely possible! She thought back on yet another coincidence. Titus at the play. It must be Dorcas, her determined enemy who hated her and hated the idea of her being an actress and, if she had discovered about the divorce . . . A spate of words on the subject of Dorcas Heberdeen emerged as an unintelligible "mumnph."

With a glare which earlier on had brought a reference to her "speaking eyes" from Titus, she put her hot cheek against the cool glass and stared fiercely into the darkening landscape. She remembered her old premonition regarding the harm Dorcas might wreak. Well, she had wreaked it and she suddenly was visited by yet another premonition— that it was by no means at an end. Yet what could Titus do, other than hold her against her will? A possible answer made her cheeks grow even warmer. Then she stiffened. They were turning. Looking out of the window, she could see nothing save the trunks of trees illuminated by the carriage lamps, but they were off the main road, she was sure of that. Were they approaching the manor?

With an omniscience which caused her to start, Titus observed, "Yes, my love, we are skirting the village of Melton Mobray. Another two miles and we should be at Renard Manor and out of danger from 'ighwaymen."

She restrained an impulse to hurl furious words at his head and then remembered that even had she not restrained herself, she could have done no speaking. She emitted a short, angry sigh. At least it had been meant as a sigh, but since it had issued from her nose rather than her throat, it sounded suspiciously like an undignified snort. And that made her crosser than ever, particularly since it was followed almost immediately by Titus's laugh.

"That would have done credit to the dragons, themselves, my love."

Since she could still glare, she did.

10

THE UNFAMILIAR SOUND of barking dogs awakened Thea. Opening her eyes, she blinked against the bright light streaming through the window to her right. That, too, was unfamiliar and at first she was confused. In the few seconds it took her to sit up, however, her confusion was replaced by an awareness of her situation. She was a prisoner! Resentfully she glanced about her at walls paneled in a light golden wood. She had not noticed the color of the room the previous night, nor the oil painting of an unknown woman in a headdress of half a century ago that hung over a carved mantelpiece, nor the fact that the canopy and curtains of her wide four-poster were fashioned from a flowered chintz. She did remember being given the cotton shift she was wearing. It was too large for her and must belong to Mrs. Martin, who, in addition to being the wife of the caretaker, was also housekeeper and cook. She had greeted her warmly as Milady Croydon.

Thea grimaced, wondering what Mrs. Martin would have thought had Titus carried her in. However, some moments before the post chaise had drawn to a stop in front of the long dark mass that was the Manor House, he had produced a knife and snipped her bonds. "The remote situation of this house, my dear, surrounded by miles of its own park and approached by a lonely road possibly frequented by 'igh-waymen, particularly at this hour of the night, will, I believe, keep you from dashing into the darkness as you did at Vauxhall," he had said mockingly. He would have rubbed her benumbed wrists and ankles had she not pushed him away.

She had not ever contemplated escape. She had returned the housekeeper's greeting politely if not cordially. She had also partaken of a small repast provided by the woman. If Mrs. Martin were surprised at the unexpected arrival of his lordship, she seemed to do his bidding with an unmitigated delight which had expanded to include his lady—and spoke well for his dealings with servants.

She flushed as she recalled his accompanying her up a wide staircase to the chamber she now occupied. Opening her door to allow her to enter, he had said, as she hesitated, "My ancestor, the Baron, would have remained . . . but since I am more civilized, I will leave you to your own devices."

She had not responded. Eight hours of mingled fright and fury coupled with the motion of the vehicle had left her too weary to do other than silently nod and close the door. Sally, coming to help her undress before going to her own bed, had been dismissed, she being in no mood to listen to the girl's comments of the horrifying events of the day. She recalled that she half expected to hear the click of a key in the lock, but she had not.

The barking of the dogs which had awakened her grew louder. It seemed to alternate between menace and a yipping hysteria, depending, she guessed on the size of the animal contributing to the chorus. She also heard the sound of wheels on the gravel and understood the reason for the canine excitement. Slipping from bed, she moved to the window, seeing before her a wide semicircle of a driveway enclosing a stretch of bright green lawn dotted with topiary trees clipped in geometrical shapes. Two hounds and a terrier were running toward a post chaise rounding the driveway. Glimpsing the coachman's face, she caught at a drapery to steady herself. She recognized him as the man who had driven herself and her aunt to Birmingham. She did not need to see the coat of arms on its panel to realize that the Marquis of Fearing had unaccountably learned of her whereabouts. A quick glance at the mantelpiece showed her that it was bare of a clock but the sun was high in the sky. It must be close to noon. He must have started for Leicestershire only a few hours after Titus himself had gone. Her thoughts veered away from that as she saw a horseman at the far end of the driveway—Titus! He must have been out riding and witnessed the Marquis's arrival.

There was a throbbing in her throat. "No, no, no," she found herself repeating as she stood transfixed at her window, unable to turn away. "He will kill him. Clive will challenge him . . . his will be the choice of weapons . . . he'll choose swords and . . ." She had an impulse to run downstairs and prevent Titus from coming any closer, or begging the Marquis to flee! There would be time to do neither, nor would she be heeded! Half sobbing, she watched the post chaise come to a stop. Almost before that happened, the Marquis had flung open his door and leaped out. He was followed by a tall man in black. She wondered who he might be, but stopped wondering because Titus had reached them and dismounting, came up to them, leading his horse by the reins. Breathlessly Thea watched as he turned toward Fearing and then she cried out, for as quick as Titus had faced him, the Marquis had struck him across the cheek and

Titus stepped back, his horse rearing and plunging because of his sudden movement. His face, she could see, was darkly flushed.

"No . . . no . . . no," she murmured a second time. Rushing to her armoire, she dragged out her garments and dressed as quickly as she could, cursing the tiny buttons at the back of her gown and at length ignoring them. Not even stopping to thrust her feet into her slippers, she was down the stairs and into the hall. At first she did not see the front door, but she found it and pulled it open. She came out onto the colonnaded porch in time to hear angry voices speaking in unison so that she could not hear what they were saying. The man in black, looking grave, stood aside, listening but saying nothing.

She dashed down the steps, not even aware of the sharp bite of the gravel on her bare feet as she came up to the Marquis. "No, no, no," she gasped. "I saw from my window. You must not fight."

"Thea," he caught her by the shoulders. "Oh, my God, has he harmed you?"

"No, I am not harmed, I am safe. Oh, I pray you, Clive, do not fight him. I am ready to go back." She looked down at herself and blushed, becoming aware of her bare feet and her wrinkled gown. "I—I did not stop to d-dress," she babbled. "Please, please, you must not fight."

"I beg your pardon, my dear," Titus said through gritted teeth. He touched his cheek. "I am not one to bear insult without retaliation."

"And you will have your retaliation, I assure you," the Marquis said coldly. "Yours is the choice—swords or pistols? I have brought them both."

"No," Thea cried, "you'll kill him." She clutched the Marquis's hand. "Do you not know that Titus is a master swordsman, that he has instructed others in that art? I pray you will not think of engaging with him."

The Marquis's eyes softened. "I am moved by your concern, my Thea, but this action in abducting you I cannot forgive. He must be punished for it and I might tell you that though I have never been an instructor in the art, I am thought to have some skill with a sword."

She turned back to Titus, "You cannot..." she began, but the words died in her throat at the look of hurt in his eyes. It was gone in an instant, leaving them stony and cold. He said, "You do not want me to slay your lover? Well, take heart, perhaps it is I who will please you and die."

"It...it would not please me," she gasped. "Oh, why must either of you think of dying? I have sustained no harm. I am not worthy of this action. No one is worth a life." She whirled back to the Marquis. "It's true...please, please do not fight, either of you." Burying her face in her hands, she burst into tears.

"My dear," it was the Marquis who put an arm around her shaking shoulders, "cannot you see? It is too late to draw back—it is a point of honor."

"Honor," she cried loudly, "damn honor. Your lives mean more to me than honor."

Shaking his head, Fearing turned resolutely back to Titus. "I passed a place by the trees," he pointed in the direction of the gatehouse. "It seems as good a dueling ground as any. Shall we seek it—or would you prefer to rest? You have been riding, you must be tired."

"As must you, my lord, traveling this long distance. No, I know the spot to which you refer and it will suffice. I will have my caretaker second me." He glanced to one side, and for the first time Thea saw that Martin had come up and was standing staring at them anxiously. "Who will you choose?" Titus continued, looking inquiringly at the man in black.

"Your pardon that I have not introduced my companion," the Marquis said. "This is Dr. Christopher Dunstan. He is a fine physician and will officiate so that we can keep this sorry matter between us."

"I must congratulate you upon your forethought," Titus visited a brief smile on the physician. "Your servant, Dr.

Dunstan—but not your patient, I pray. I welcome you t
my house."

Dr. Dunstan bowed slightly, "I thank you, my lord
though I wish that neither of you were embarked upon thi
dangerous course."

"Having had your say, come with us," Titus returned
"and since my lord has enlisted no second, neither shall I
but hold, one more duty before I go." Crossing to Martin
he murmured something in a voice so low Thea could no
catch it, though she was standing near them. Turning back,
he bowed to the Marquis. "I am at your service, Fearing.'

The Marquis looked at him grimly. "And I am at yours
No." He raised his hand as Thea stepped forward. "I charge
you, my dear, do not accompany us."

"I shall," she cried, and then started as Martin seized her
arm.

"I am sorry, milady," he said, "but the master does no
wish it."

She struggled against that iron grip, striving to free herself. "Let me go," she cried desperately.

"No, milady," he returned stolidly. "The master does not
wish it."

Once more she was in her chamber, but the door was
locked from the outside and she had been beating against
it futilely for she did not know how long. Her face was wet
with tears, her hands and arms ached from her exertions
and from the strong pressure Martin had exerted on them
as he had dragged her into the house and at length, carried
her wailing and struggling up the stairs. He had hurriedly
deposited her in her bed, running out and slamming the door
before she had been able to reach it. She had screamed,
threatened, even cursed him—all in all, her manner had
been most undignified, but that did not concern her. Nothing
concerned her save that which was taking place on the
dueling ground.

"Please . . . please . . ." She shook the heavy door once

again and sank to her knees, resting her cheek against its panels. "Oh, God, please, please, please do not let them take any harm."

It was useless to offer up such a prayer, she knew that. They would be harmed, but not fatally. They must not either one of them die because of her. She tensed. She had heard a sound upon the stairs. Once more she cried, "I pray you let me out." She fell silent, listening. There were footsteps in the hall. They approached her door and stopped. The key was turning in the lock and the latch clicking.

She rolled out of the way as the door opened inward. Looking up at Mrs. Martin, her smiles gone, her face somber and streaked with tears, Thea leaped to her feet. "What has happened?" she cried.

"Oh, milady, come quickly, I know 'e'll want to see you afore . . ." The woman burst into sobs.

In later life Thea never remembered following Mrs. Martin down the stairs or out across the grounds or to the little stretch of grass where the physician knelt beside the fallen man. Awareness returned only when she, too, was kneeling staring down into the face of him whom she had called so briefly "husband." He was very pale and there was a huge scarlet stain on his white shirt. His eyes were closed, the long dark lashes sweeping his pale cheeks. At first it seemed to her that he was not breathing, but there was still movement, faint but perceptible, still the pulse beating at the base of his throat, still the rise and fall of his chest.

"No," Thea whispered. "No," and hardly knew she had spoken aloud. "It is not right . . . it should not—must not—cannot happen this way."

He should not be lying there; they were nearly to the end of the play—the farce, that is what it had been, a farce; she had acted in so many, where lovers quarreled with each other and were separated for five acts. One of them, usually the man, resorted to all manner of stratagems to win the woman back, but she would not heed him not until the final few minutes when all knots were unraveled. Yet all along, when she was ignoring him, teasing him, playing her tricks, all along in the back of her mind, she had known that she would forgive him in the end—because she loved him. Lydia Languish would wed Captain Absolute, Polly would be united with MacHeath, Beatrice, with Benedict. Toasts would be drunk and little songs sung and they would live happily ever after. That was how it was supposed to be; no playwright ever ended a comedy with a tragedy. No hero ever lay white and bleeding on the grass with death waiting in the wings. *Death*? But he could not die, not when she loved him so much. Yes, loved him, she knew that now and had loved him ever since she had first seen him, could love no one else, ever, ever, ever—and was he to die?

"Oh, God," she moaned in agony.

His eyes opened. He frowned as he saw her and whispered, "I told them you were not...not..."

"Shh, you must not speak."

"Must," he insisted. "Glad...here...wanted to beg pardon f-for..."

"No, please...be quiet, my love."

"Love...?" he murmered. "Love you, Anthea. Do love...you." He tried to raise his hand toward her cheek, but it fell back and his eyes closed again.

"Titus!" she whispered out of a deep horror. With an effort she managed to turn her head toward the physician. "Is he..."

"Not yet," he returned, "but the wound is deep. I fear for the lung."

A shadow was thrown across the two of them and Thea heard Fearing's voice. She raised her eyes, staring into his grave face. He said solemnly, "He fought well and bravely. He is a master, as you said and easily my match—save for an unlucky stumble. I'd not intended to kill him, but I had thrust and the point passed 'neath his guard. I could not stop it." He sighed. "I think you must soon be free, my dear—but I am sorry, I did not want it to happen thus."

"Free." Horror thrilled through her. "Free," she repeated, her voice a mere thread of sound. "If . . . he dies, Clive, I—I shall not want to live."

The Marquis of Fearing paled and stepped back. "Thea," he said in a shocked voice, "what are you telling me?"

She shook her head. She could not continue to look at him while Titus still breathed. She must keep her eyes on her husband. She looked down at him. He was still breathing, but oh, the stain on his shirt seemed to be spreading and there was blood on the ground —his life blood? A lock of his hair had fallen across his forehead and trailed into his eyes. She pushed it back gently, her finger caressing his cheek, which still bore evidence of her scratch.

Above her the Marquis said in a tight voice, "You love him."

She made the effort but could not summon enough sound to clothe her answer. "Yes," she whispered.

"My poor girl, why all your struggles against him . . . why everything?"

"I—I did not know how much I still . . . I did not know. It is too little to say I am sorry. I swear to you, I did not know. Oh, why did it come to this? How did you find him? Who told you where to—to ride?" She could not hold back the sobs that shook her.

"'Twas Lady Heberdeen, she . . . but it's not the time to explain."

"Dorcas," she uttered. Thea turned cold, remembering her early fears. Then her attention was once more upon her husband's face. Had he grown paler? She addressed the physician, "Is there a chance?"

"I cannot say, milady. We must wait."

"Wait," she repeated, thinking that if words were made of substances, "wait" must be fashioned from iron. She stared at Dr. Dunstan and thought that the Angel of Death must have eyes similar to those calm, contemplative, steady

orbs. Eyes which promised nothing in the way of hope—
the gaze of one who waits patiently until life's final breath
is drawn.

"Guilia, Guilia, Guilia," the sick man muttered and
moved restlessly only to be caught gently in a determined
grasp and held while a soft cool cloth was applied to his
burning forehead.

"Guilia," he moaned again.

"*Cara mia*," Thea whispered, employing the term he had
repeated so often during his delirium. She was not jealous
of Guilia, for as often as he had called on his dead wife,
he had cried, "Anthea ... Anthea..." and begged her to
come back to him. Through his fevered babbling she had
learned of his endless searching for her. She had also heard
him talking wildly to someone seen only in his clouded
mind. "She is not here?" he had questioned intently. "You
have never heard of an Anthea Croy—she may call herself
Heberdeen." And then there were the painful times when
he had begged her not to be dead and sharing Guilia's grave.

"Shall not have her..." He moved restlessly again.
"Fearing shall not—so many wenches, prizing none of
them—shall not have her...mine. Love her...love
her."

"And I love you," she whispered into his unheeding ears.
"So much. Why did I not know, my heart's darling, why
did I not know?"

That same question had often hovered on Dolly Playfaire's lips as she watched her niece's long vigil at her
husband's bedside. It was eight days since a grim-faced
Marquis of Fearing had arrived at her cottage to give her
a brief summary of the events which had taken place two
days earlier—and to beg her to pack such necessities as she
believed Thea must require and, if possible, to return with
him to Leicestershire.

Fortunately she had been able to come. Though the Marquis had prepared her for Thea's distress, she had not ex-

pected to find her in such agony of mind. Though she had been much concerned over her, she had also been exasperated. All her misery, everything could have been avoided if she had only known her own heart. Yet she could not fault Thea for the bitterness which had spurred most of her actions. Even a girl less sensitive than her niece would have been hurt by Titus's behavior on their wedding night. And, of course, there had been Rosalie Croydon's confidence to match it. Yet, if she had remained to face her groom . . . But she had not, and perhaps it might not have sufficed, for he had been still grieving over his Guilia. The fact was that neither of them had been prepared for the marriage which Lady Cornelia had helped to bring about. However, there must have been some attraction on his side, a seed planted that had flowered immediately he had seen Thea again. As for Thea, her ability to keep Fearing at arm's length for such a long time, was also explained.

Actually Fearing was the real sufferer in this situation. He had been kindness itself since the day of the duel. Yet Dolly found she could not entirely pity him. Despite his arguments to the contrary, she was quite convinced that in his eagerness to avoid a divorce, he had been determined to slay the man who stood in his way. She did not quite believe his story about being unable to stay his weapon when his opponent stumbled and dropped his guard. She sighed. It little mattered now.

The wound was less dangerous than they had feared. It had grazed but not punctured the lung, but, as so often happened, fever had developed, and for the last five days Titus had been delirious. She firmed her lips. In her opinion Dr. Dunstan, fine physician though he was, had not used the proper treatment. He had refused to bleed his patient and, as everyone knew, that was the time-honored method of quelling a fever. She had begged her niece to ask for another opinion, but Thea had refused.

"Oh, Aunt!"

Dolly started and turned to find Thea at her side, her

eyes filled with tears. Through stiff lips she asked, "Child, what has happened. Is he . . . ?"

"No, I beg you will fetch Dr. Dunstan. The fever has gone and he is sleeping peacefully at last. See." Thea glided to the mantelpiece and was back with a candle.

Moving quickly to the bed, Dolly held the candle over Titus's face. For a moment her heart seemed to stop. He lay so still. But a second glance showed her that he was breathing and, touching his forehead, she found it cool. Tears rose to her own eyes. "It is true. I shall fetch the physician immediately."

"It is true," Dr. Dunstan repeated Dolly's words. He added, "He will begin to improve now."

Dr. Dunstan was smiling. He was not an Angel of Death, Thea thought ecstatically. He had proved to be the giver of life!

Dreams. There had been so many of them and the most persistent of them was the most unbelievable, the presence of Anthea in his room, but, of course, she had gone with Fearing. Titus's eyes dwelt on Mrs. Martin, dozing by his bed. It was she who had tended him he knew, and he was grateful to her though, at the same time, he would not have minded quitting this life, complicated as it was by his mistakes. The last one had been the worst. He had abducted Anthea because on the night of the masquerade it had seemed to him that she had responded to him. He winced at the memory of her terror for the Marquis, of her warning that he would be dueling with a master. She need not have worried; the Marquis had proved his match and more. Of course, if he had not stumbled . . . He shook his head slightly. If only he had not been so weary! He had been on horseback since dawn and he had slept very little the night before. That was not surprising considering the enormity of his action in seizing her. He had been pondering on the situation, pondering on what he must say to her when she awakened, and he had finally decided upon an approach.

Then, returning to the manor, he had seen the Marquis of Fearing's post chaise.

It was amazing that he had not died. There had been no pain at first, but there had been a terrible weakness. He was still feeling weak. But at least the dreams were gone, the dreams and a persistent nightmare. He had been in a place of twilight, of leaden skies and gray earth. Strange trees with twisted trunks and branches which had seemed to writhe with a life of their own grew amidst massive stones which, while they had no lettering upon them, he knew to be gravestones. Among them moved spectral shapes, which, on being touched, floated off like blown dandelion seeds. One had remained to confront him and he had known it must be Guilia, beckoning him to follow. He had wanted to follow—yet, at the same time, had been reluctant. Then, something had held him back, a voice. It had begged him not to die and he had heeded it, because it seemed to him that he knew its cadences, but now that consciousness had returned... He sighed. "It—could not be."

Mrs. Martin awakened immediately and looked down at him. "M-my lord, you spoke? Are ye awake, then?" she questioned in tremulous tones.

"Yes," he managed a smile. "I am awake. And I know it was you looked after me. I thank you..."

She rose quickly. "I've 'elped, my lord."

To his amazement she sped from the room. It was, he thought, odd behavior for one who was tending the sick. Usually they were more concerned, too concerned, wanting to bring you more pillows, press water or soup to your lips. He was hungry, ravenously hungry, but she had not even asked him how he felt. Of course she was not a real nurse and no doubt she did not understand. He felt a draught of cold air. The door must have opened and she was returning, but... He had managed to turn his head and it was not she. His eyes widened—could he still be lost in his twilight landscape? There was a white-clad wraith approaching his bed. It knelt at his side and would it float away? Looking into its face, he breathed, "Anthea..."

"Yes, dearest," she said softly. "Mrs. Martin told me you'd awakened."

Her hand was smoothing his hair back from his forehead. It was cool and he recalled the touch. Had it prevented him from remaining in the twilight land? It was such a thin hand, almost transparent, but it was real. She was real, but so pale. "I dreamed you were with me," he told her, "but I thought 'twas but a dream. You and Fearing...?"

Her fingers trailed gently across his lips. "No."

Her eyes were enormous in her wasted contenance. Concernedly he said, "You have been ill."

"No."

"You're so pale."

"It is fashionable to be pale," she said teasingly.

She was still stroking his hair. He remembered that, remembered her gentleness and recognized the voice which he had believed a part of his dreams. "It was you with me, Anthea."

"Yes, my love."

"Love... do you love me?"

The blue eyes were brimming with tears. They spilled down the pale cheeks as she confessed, "Oh, yes, my heart's darling, I do. But now, you must sleep."

He did not want to sleep. There were so many questions he wanted to ask her, so many things he wanted to tell her. He was filled with such happiness—but his eyelids were heavy. He slept.

The large traveling coach carrying Lady Cornelia toward the village of Melton Mobray was moving faster than usual. Her ladyship was on her way to visit her son Titus, injured in a riding accident.

She was accompanied by her daughter-in-law, Lady Rosalie Croydon, and though the coach could have easily accommodated their two abigails, these women were in a second coach which also contained luggage and the monogrammed sheets which her ladyship preferred to those furnished by the inns at which they stopped.

It had been a long and, as far as Rosalie was concerned, a very tedious journey. Lady Cornelia was never a good companion since she either dominated the conversation or she slept. Rosalie never minded her sleeping. Even though she snored loudly, that noise was preferable to her complaints about the coachman's driving, the county's neglect of the roads, and the terrible accommodations they might expect or had received at what were erroneously called first-class inns.

However, on this occasion these topics had been abandoned for one which minimized every other horror her ladyship had been forced to endure throughout a long life. Even the possibility that her son might have been badly hurt took second place to the terrible discovery that had occupied Lady Cornelia's mind ever since Lady Heberdeen had forwarded to her a copy of the *Morning Post* of two weeks earlier. The item that Lady Heberdeen had underlined with a force that had left a hole in the paper concerned Lady Anthea Croydon or, as she was known to a large public in the English provinces and at Drury Lane, Thea Playfaire!

The only comfort that Rosalie derived from Lady Cornelia's unceasing diatribe was that she, herself, was in a sense exonerated from the crime of having divulged the story of Guilia di Rossi to that "*creature*" as Lady Cornelia now called Anthea.

"I have never been so shocked," breathed Lady Cornelia, breaking a short silence and saying much the same thing she had been saying ever since leaving Vane. "That wretched journal. How dared they print such an item. And to use names rather than initials so that all the Polite World knows that my poor boy is wed to an actress! I vow they might as well have said 'trull,' for it is one and the same thing."

"It was said that she was a great success at Drury Lane," Rosalie remarked.

"Am I to understand that you are praising her for her folly?" Lady Cornelia demanded.

"No, I was only saying..." Rosalie began.

"That a female in her position should demean herself in such a manner," Lady Cornelia rasped. "I hope and pray that my poor boy does not know of it. If he is yet ill, I am sure the knowledge must impede his recovery. Despite his earlier wildness, he has settled down and there's no disputing his pride in his name." She glared at Rosalie. "I hope that on this occasion, you will have the goodness to hold your tongue."

Rosalie flushed. "I shall say nothing, of course."

"No one must say anything until he is recovered, but then we will have to consider what we must do about that wretched chit. If I might have spoken to her brother—not that I blame him for going to Brighton. I am sure that he and his poor little wife could not wait to get out of town. Oh, it passes all understanding. How could she have done it? How dared one who bore the name of Vane lower herself to such a degree?"

Rosalie, looking out of the window, hoped devoutly that they would soon reach Renard Manor, for then her mother-in-law must abandon the subject of Anthea Croydon. For herself, she wondered why Titus had come to this particular dwelling. She knew that he had never liked it. And how had he, an excellent horseman, a regular centaur in the saddle Odo had called him, how had he sustained an injury bad enough to keep him bedded and unable to communicate with his mother for a month? That did not seem to concern Lady Cornelia at all. Of course, it was true that Titus often went off on long journeys without informing anyone as to his destination, but generally he did write. Perhaps it was foolish to worry about him, but she did. She was fond of him and, she thought with a streak of defiance, she was also fond of Anthea. She could not approve her going on the stage, but, at the same time, she could not but admire the girl for her daring. It was certainly better for them to know she was successful in her profession than to fear she was living in sad seclusion or, worse yet, lying at the bottom of a river.

"I had rather," Lady Cornelia broke the short silence that had fallen between them by intoning, "learned that she were at the bottom of the sea!"

Though the garden at Renard Manor did not have the vast proportions of its counterpart at Vane, it was still charming. Mrs. Martin had spent a great deal of her time putting in new plants. She had had the cooperation of the three gardeners, all of whom admired one whose thumb was obviously green. The results of her efforts were to be seen in roses of all colors, from white to flaming scarlet. In the midst of these rosebeds stood a small summer house and it was here that Titus liked to sit while Thea read to him from his favorite Shakespearean plays.

His health was much improved, but he was still shaky and his face yet retained a transparent look that moved his wife to declare he must rest as much as possible. Though under all other circumstances he would have protested mightily at such arbitrary strictures, the delight he took in her company rendered him, in the words of Mrs. Martin, "as docile as a lamb."

"La," she had remarked to Dolly Playfaire, "I never seen 'im so 'appy an' 'er, too. Like two turtledoves they is."

If that sentiment was badly overworked, it was also extremely apt. In common with Richard II, they had "written sorrow upon the bosom of the earth," but unlike that unhappy King, they had been given the opportunity to erase it and having done so, were the more joyful.

Dolly was watching them now and wishing she had a knack for sketching, for surely they would have made a lovely picture, he in his chair and she at his feet with the great leather book open on her lap. She had come with some trifling question but, she decided, she would not disturb them yet.

"Oh, Mrs. Playfaire," Mrs. Martin came quickly through the garden, her eyes distressed and her lips trembling. "It's 'erself an' . . ." She broke off as Lady Cornelia stalked past her, coming to an abrupt stop and turning fiery eyes upon Thea.

"What is that abandoned creature doing here in my son's establishment?" she demanded loudly.

"Oh, please," a nervous young woman caught up with her. "Do not disturb them."

"No, you must not . . ." Dolly put out a hand to halt Lady Cornelia's onward rush but was brushed aside as if she had been an importunate servant.

"Oh, dear, she is going to be horrid," mourned the young woman. "And they did look so happy and peaceful."

"I see she is," Dolly muttered between clenched teeth. She hurried after Lady Cornelia.

She was in time to hear her say, "You are to leave at once, Anthea, or whatever you now call yourself. I do not know what you are doing here, but you are no longer welcome in this house nor any other establishment belonging to the Vanes."

"Mother," Titus started to rise.

"No," Thea clasped his hand, gently pulling him down. "Please, my love."

Lady Cornelia's face was flushed. She moved closer to Thea. "I have never been so shocked, so horrified in all my life as when I read the *Morning Post* sent to me by your sister-in-law, who is, I might add, as shocked as myself that . . . that . . ."

"That my wife is an actress and will be appearing at Drury Lane next season," Titus finished coldly.

Lady Cornelia drew herself up to her full height and at the same time seemed actually to swell as she intoned, "I had thought you'd learned the error of your ways, but I see I was wrong. Either you are lost to all sense of Propriety or your recent illness has made you light-headed."

"I hope I am not light-headed, Mother, for I have offered

myself as Thea's manager— and have already sent a letter informing the management of Drury Lane of my intention. I assure you I will need my wits about me if I am to bargain successfully for her."

"You... You... You..." Lady Cornelia's face was turning purple when Dolly hastily thrust a hand beneath her elbow.

"Come, Cornelia, your papa died of apoplexy. If you do not wish to follow in his footsteps, I suggest you come with me and partake of a syllabub."

"You! Who are you? And how dare you address me by my given name?"

"I am Dillys Heberdeen," Dolly explained. "And I am sure you must remember me—or at least my late sister, Harriet, with whom you were well acquainted."

"Dillys Heberdeen!" Lady Cornelia looked as if she were about to succumb to the apoplexy Dolly had mentioned. "But you are d-d-dead."

"No, though perhaps you might call me thus... since I too am an actress."

"It was you..." Lady Cornelia pointed a shaking finger at her. "You who..."

"Indeed, it was and I am sure you would like to hear more of the pertinent details." Dolly's grasp on Lady Cornelia's arm tightened. "And I am quite willing to tell them to you over a syllabub, which I am sure Mrs. Martin will be delighted to make." She began to propel Lady Cornelia toward the house. Being evidently too shocked to resist, the lady went as docilely as the lamb to which Mrs. Martin had compared Titus, with Rosalie trailing behind her—but not before the young woman had dared to wink at the couple in the summer house.

"How... how did your aunt manage that?" Titus demanded once his laughter had subsided.

"She can be most persuasive when she chooses and I think your mother's curiosity was piqued. They knew each other when young." She broke off and gave him a quizzical look. "I must say, my dear love, that you did not need to add fuel to her fires by telling her such outrageous falsehoods."

"Falsehoods?" He raised his eyebrows. "I was trained and very painfully, too, never to tell a falsehood to my mother."

"Come," she smiled at him fondly, "you cannot mean that you wish me to return to the stage!"

"Do you not wish it?" he countered.

"I wish only to be your wife."

"And I appreciate the sacrifice but will not accept it. I have the greatest desire to see your Juliet, your Portia, and your Rosalind upon the stage at Drury Lane, but not unless I manage you."

On a night in October 1818, an audience at Drury Lane, which had been all whispers, rustles, titters, and shocked glances at the beginning of the performance was quiet and hushed as it listened to the slender young woman standing alone on stage. She was nearing the end of Rosalind's epilogue, "'If I were a woman I would kiss as many of you as had beards that pleased me, complexions that liked me and breaths that I defied not: and, I am sure, as many as have good beards or good faces or sweet breaths will, for my kind offer, when I make curtsy, bid me farewell.' "

There was a hush as she bowed and stepped behind the curtain—then the storm broke with the lightning and thunder of cheers and applause.

The tall handsome man who had waited in the wings throughout the play, joined another who had taken a chair in that same area. Together they came into the dressing room where Rosalind was prosaically removing her makeup. Seeing their glowing faces in the glass, she turned and held out her arms, kissing first her husband and then her brother. However, she was seen to frown as her husband said, "I must go to the greenroom to mingle with your public—

accepting and spreading the good word."

She regarded him anxiously. "I do not like to think of you acting in such a capacity. After all, my love, you are . . ."

"Your husband," he concluded, "and I might tell you that I have worked as a horse trainer, a tutor, a fencing master, and none of these occupations gave me such rewards as I have received by becoming your manager." Dropping a kiss on her head, he moved from the room. Her brother lingered.

"Well, Bertie," she smiled mistily, "tell me where I went wrong. As you know, Aunt Dolly's usually my mentor but she is in Bath as Mrs. Malaprop."

"If she were here, I am sure she would find no fault with your performance. You were even better than last summer and I should not have thought that possible."

"Alas, I see you are no critic when it comes to your sister. But I am glad to see you here. I had not known you were back in town until Titus told me at the end of the first act." Pausing, she then added diffidently, "I expect Dorcas is not with you?"

He regarded her gravely. "Nor will she be ever again."

"Oh," she said, distressed, "I had not thought . . ."

"I pray you'll not give any thought to it now. Suffice to say I am not unhappy."

"And she?"

He shrugged. "How might I know? I expect she finds Brighton pleasant enough. Her parents are with her and no doubt fill her ears with my inadequacies, whenever she, herself waxes silent on them. I am sure that must give her a pleasure of sorts, but it cannot equal mine in being apart from her."

"But I fear it was I brought trouble to you."

"Never—I knew within six months of our marriage that we were unsuited and am delighted that she gave me reason enough to effect a separation."

"Is that the truth?" She stared into his eyes.

He returned her gaze steadily. "I hope you are satisfied with what you read."

"Oh, Bertie, yes." She held out her arms.

It was late when Thea and Titus left the feast given them by the Marquis of Fearing and the exquisite young woman who acted as his hostess and whom he proudly introduced as Miss Zenobia from the Corps de Ballet at Covent Garden. Yet once they were in their own chamber at Dolly's cottage where they were staying while their own house in the village of Chelsea was being completed, they lay sleepless, staring at the graying embers in the fireplace.

It seemed to Titus that his wife was regarding him a little anxiously. He wondered if she were still worried over her performance. He knew her well enough by now to realize that she was a perfectionist. He said, "It was a very fine beginning to your season, my love."

She replied hesitantly, "It was not a beginning, Titus, it was an ending."

"An ending!" he exclaimed. "What can you mean?"

"I have wanted to tell you for at least a month," she spoke quickly, "but I thought I would wait until after to-night. I pray you'll not frown on me for waiting—but Dr. Dunstan assured me that it would be safe for me to go on."

"Safe?" he repeated.

"My love, as my manager I expect you must be the first to know that I am retiring for the rest of this season. Since we have heard that your mama has gone to live at the Dower House, I am quite determined that we must repair to the country and live at Vane for the next few months—for that is where I want our child to be born."

He clutched her to him convulsively, saying in a low, worried voice, "You'll not tell me . . ."

"Yes, love, I shall tell you that I am breeding. It has actually been close to six weeks that I have known it! I beg that you'll not be frightened, for Dr. Dunstan assures me that I am in perfect health. He tells me, too, that it will probably be a boy."

"I do not see how he can determine that, my dearest," he murmured between kisses showered upon her face.

"I think, my love, he reasons, as your mother has, that since I had two brothers and five uncles and..."

She was not able to continue with her numbering because her husband had indignantly silenced her with another, longer kiss.

Epilogue

IT WAS THE last act of *Othello* and the audience at Drury Lane was silent—though of course there were the usual coughs from gentlemen who hoped that these would conceal their emotions while their female companions openly wept. Charles Kemble, the Othello, crawled toward the bed wherein lay the body of his strangled wife, her golden hair flowing artistically over the pillows. He murmured in a voice choked with sobs, but which was heard five tiers of seats up, "I...kissed thee ere I killed thee, no way but this...killing myself to...die upon a kiss."

He fell back near the bed—but not quite close enough to reach the limp hand of his dead wife. As he tried and tried again to touch those cold fingers, a prolonged howl— it sounded like a baby!—issued from the wings. It was followed by an unmistakable titter from the audience. Kemble's fists clenched and the look he darted at his supine victim was more murderous than any he had employed even while strangling her. Within seconds, he had twitched, gasped, sighed and died.

Moments later the curtain fell but, as Kemble and his leading lady took their bows, the actors' smiles were less than cordial. Without one look at his co-star, Kemble strode offstage to his dressing room.

Entering her own dressing room, the Desdemona found her husband tickling a cooing and currently good-humored baby. For a second she was deflected from what she had wanted to say. It was always a delight to see Titus so happy—for the months before she had given birth, he had been moody and fearful, looking at her as if he thought every day might be her last. His relief at the ease with which his heir had come into the world had been great. However, it was incumbent upon her to say, as she did now and with a slight shake of the head, "My love, I told you we should wait before bringing him into the wings. Kemble was furious at the noise and the laughter."

Titus lifted adoring eyes from his son to fasten a no less adoring glance upon his wife. "Nonsense, my dearest Thea, it was not the noise or the laughter that galled Kemble."

"Was it not?" she demanded. "What was it, then?"

"'T'was the idea of being upstaged by a professional," he said proudly.

There's nothing more precious than your

Second Chance at Love ™

◦ Second Chance at Love ◦
™

_____ 05623-5 **WINDS OF MORNING #13** Laurie Marath

_____ 05704-5 **HARD TO HANDLE #14** Susanna Collins

_____ 06067-4 **BELOVED PIRATE #15** Margie Michaels

_____ 05978-1 **PASSION'S FLIGHT #16** Marilyn Mathieu

_____ 05847-5 **HEART OF THE GLEN #17** Lily Bradford

_____ 05977-3 **BIRD OF PARADISE #18** Winter Ames

_____ 05705-3 **DESTINY'S SPELL #19** Susanna Collins

_____ 06106-9 **GENTLE TORMENT #20** Johanna Phillips

_____ 06059-3 **MAYAN ENCHANTMENT #21** Lila Ford

_____ 06301-0 **LED INTO SUNLIGHT #22** Claire Evans

_____ 06131-X **CRYSTAL FIRE #23** Valerie Nye

_____ 06150-6 **PASSION'S GAMES #24**
Meredith Kingston

_____ 06160-3 **GIFT OF ORCHIDS #25** Patti Moore

_____ 06108-5 **SILKEN CARESSES #26** Samantha Carroll

_____ 06318-5 **SAPPHIRE ISLAND #27** Diane Crawford

All of the above titles are $1.75 per copy

Available at your local bookstore or return this form to:

SECOND CHANCE AT LOVE
The Berkley/Jove Publishing Group
200 Madison Avenue, New York, New York 10016

**Please enclose 50¢ for postage and handling for one book, 25¢
each add'l book ($1.25 max.). No cash, CODs or stamps. Total
amount enclosed: $_____ in check or money order.**

NAME _____

ADDRESS _____

CITY _____ STATE/ZIP _____

Allow six weeks for delivery.

SK-41

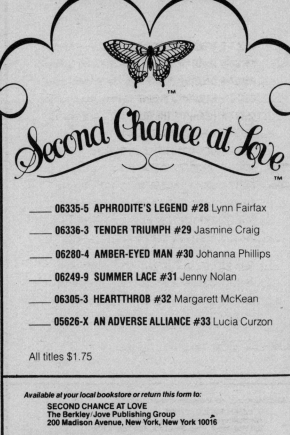